FROM THE SEA TO THE STARS

MOON CRUSHER PART 3

SUSAN KITE

This is a work of fiction. Names, characters, places, and incidents are products of the author's imagination or are used fictitiously and are not to be construed as real. Any resemblance to actual events, locations, organizations, or persons, living or dead, is entirely coincidental.

World Castle Publishing, LLC

Pensacola, Florida

Copyright © 2025 Susan Kite

Hardback ISBN: 9798300535438

Paperback ISBN: 9798891263154

eBook ISBN: 9798891263161

First Edition World Castle Publishing, LLC, January 14, 2025

http://www.worldcastlepublishing.com

Licensing Notes

Cover: Cover Designs by Karen

Cover-designs-by-karen.com

Editor: Karen Fuller

Thanks to my wonderful husband, Dan, my first fan. Also to my children, Danielle and Thomas, my second fans. I love you to the moon and back!

CHAPTER ONE

Diego Perez knew his reptilian commander, Ziron, was furious when he snarled, showing all sixty-six-pointed teeth. The young sub-commander, lower class, realized he wasn't the reason, despite his tendency to blow up things and get into trouble. The Supreme Commander of the Seressin Empire recently acknowledged his part in frustrating a Resh assassination plot. No time to get into trouble since then.

Something in the message Commander Ziron just received upset him. He growled something under his breath, but Diego wasn't about to ask him to repeat the curse. The fifteen-year-old human continued his study of the navigational computer.

A tremendous roar shook the bridge.

"Commander?" The feline Grrlock, Hreeshan, asked. He manned the station overlooking the ship's systems.

"After all we've accomplished, why does the Supreme Commander feel inspired to send me on a diplomatic run to Amashi? Does he hate me that much?" Ziron growled.

Hreeshan's whiskers shook, and his ears twitched. The Grrlock had problems keeping a straight face.

Diego's curiosity got the best of him. "Marix, what is Amashi?"

"Probably the wettest, least desirable, deadest planet in the empire," Ziron growled.

"Wet, sir?"

"It's a water planet. Ninety-five percent oceans and seas. Barely enough land area to build a spaceport and administrative offices," Ziron continued. "Pull up the coordinates for Amashi."

Diego typed the name of the planet into the computer and

waited. It didn't take long. A page appeared telling him about
the planet and its system. It showed small thumbnail pictures
of various places on the planet. Almost everything was under
water except the spaceport. The sky was a very striking shade
of bluish-green, and one picture showed a brilliant sunset of a
smaller reddish-orange sun. Diego gave Commander Ziron the
coordinates, then added. "It appears to be a very peaceful and
beautiful planet, Marix."

Ziron grunted, and Hreeshan's soft, mewing chuckle told
Diego he may have said too much.

"Perhaps you'd like to visit our most illustrious vacation
spot."

Diego didn't pick up on the tone. "Oh, is it a place where
people vacation?"

"Tell me, quirlis, if a dry desert planet denizen would
enjoy a water-covered world." He paused. "It seems to me there
was much water near where you lived on your planet."

"Uh, no, sir. I guess you wouldn't enjoy that. And yes,
my home planet had places of dry land and ocean places." The
pictures were enticing, and he added, "If you want me to go to
Amashi in your place... I mean, if you think I could do the job,
Marix Ziron..."

Ziron laughed. "You have blown up a moon, defeated
the Resh in their home system, and helped the Seressin Empire
grow by another planet.... And Amashi is the most boring and
unpleasant planet in the most uninspiring star-system in the
empire. I believe you could handle the job. I have the diplomatic
scroll from the Supreme Commander. Anaar can teach you the
other information you need."

Now that Ziron had a way out of the assignment, he acted
jovial—for a Seressin.

"Will I go alone, sir?"

"You will have a small crew on your ship. They will be

your delegation on this mission. Please try not to destroy the ship." Ziron smiled as Diego blushed in embarrassment.

"Yes, sir. I will do my best. Uh, I won't destroy the ship."

Ziron gave another full-throated laugh. "Take a few of the Turengen. They will most likely enjoy Amashi."

"I agree, sir. The otter-like Turengen would love it."

"Perhaps my cousins would like to go as well," Hreeshan suggested with a smile.

"I planned on asking them," Diego replied.

———

"Yes, Diego. I would love to go to Amashi," Bress said. "I can choose others to be crewmembers on your ship. How many days will we be there?"

"Commander Ziron gave me some leeway. The actual duties take three days. But he said I could spend longer on the planet if I wanted. He said eight days, not counting the time traveling there and back. If you think two others can handle systems on the scout ship, then choose. You have been their teacher. I am going to ask Rreengrol and Rrishan if they will come."

"Better make it an assignment."

"Why wouldn't they want to come?"

"They are Grrlocks. Not sure they like water as much as Turengens."

"Oh. I won't force them, but I hope they'll come. They took me to the ocean on Grrlock." He sighed. "I guess I'd better talk to them. I'll let you know when we are departing."

He found Rreengrol working out with a pair of Breanths and his sister. Diego decided he needed exercise as well. He pulled out an anfrees, the bladed staff that served as a favorite for workouts.

"I am surprised the marix has given you time to come and practice," Rreengrol said. "Let's see how much you've forgotten."

"Look who's talking, my friend. I noticed on the roster that you haven't been here for several weeks."

Rreengrol laughed as he took up the challenge. "Now we find out whose muscles are the flabbiest." He raised his anfrees in salute, and Diego did the same.

"Go!" the Grrlock shouted. The staves whirled, clicked, and clacked together too fast to see.

Tight muscles told Diego he had neglected his martial arts practice, but his body eased into a cadence, and his muscles slid into the maneuvers. He pushed the blunt end of the anfrees into Rreengrol's midsection a time or two, but his friend whacked him against the side of his head once and tripped him up. Points tallied on a wall-mounted scoreboard for the various hits and defensive moves.

Finally, Rrishan called a halt. "It's almost curfew, and I haven't trained yet."

Diego was more than glad to end the bout, ready to collapse on the mat. "That was a great session, Rreengrol," he choked out as he tried filling his lungs.

"The score bears that out," the Grrlock replied, panting. "We need to do that more often."

"We will if you accept an assignment I have for you," Diego returned.

"Assignment?"

"Yes, for you and Rrishan. I asked Bress, and he's selecting a couple of Turengen to come with us."

"Where?" Rreengrol asked, wiping his anfrees and storing it away.

Rrishan's eyes sparkled in anticipation. "I get to go, too? Will we be fighting Resh?"

Diego laughed. "Yes, and no. Commander Hreeshan suggested I ask you, but Bress said you two wouldn't be eager for such an assignment. So, I'm making it voluntary."

"Where?" Rreengrol repeated.

"Amashi. A routine diplomatic visit. We'll be gone for two weeks," Diego began. "I was told it would be a plus on our records to make such a visit."

Rrishan looked confused. "I have never heard of Amashi. If it's not dangerous, then what is this place's significance?"

"It's the Seressin's favorite pleasure planet," Rreengrol said.

"Huh?" Rrishan frowned. "Would someone please tell me more about Amashi?"

Rreengrol laughed. "It's a planet almost completely covered with water. Pretty much all the life forms live underwater."

"You already know about it?" Diego asked Rreengrol.

"Sure. The only reason Amashi is in the Seressin Empire is because it sits in the middle of a quadrant containing some important systems."

"Commander Ziron wasn't happy about being assigned to visit Amashi."

"Of course not," Rreengrol replied with a laugh. "He comes from a desert planet."

"Want to come with me or not?"

"Sure, I do!" Rrishan answered. "It will be interesting seeing so much water."

"And to get your furry little feet wet," Rreengrol teased.

"I don't mind. I enjoy seeing new places. That's one reason I wanted to sign up as a squire," she retorted.

Diego gazed anxiously at his friend. "Rreengrol?"

The Grrlock scratched under his chin. His whiskers twitched in amusement. "Oh, alright. Someone has to keep you two in line."

Diego grinned. "Great!"

"When are we leaving?" Rrishan asked.

"In four days," he replied.

"And in what ship?" Rreengrol asked.

"One of the commander's scout ships. Not the newest one, but a capable one."

"In case you destroy something again," Rreengrol quipped.

"Ha, ha! Perhaps."

"Okay, which one of you is going to do a round with me?" Rrishan asked, her anfrees at ready.

Diego laughed, feeling his muscles stiffening. "Which one of us do you think might survive another bout?"

Rrishan looked at her wristwatch in disgust. "Kitten fluff! It's time for junior squires to retire. You two owe me next time."

"Gladly, and I will knock your whiskers off," Diego replied in Grrlock.

"When cats live in the ocean," she replied with a Grrlock saying.

Diego thought that might happen, considering where they were going.

CHAPTER TWO

Diego's anxiety level increased as the days passed. He inspected the spaceship with Rreengrol and Bress. The systems were in top operating condition. Jeng and Fress, the two Turengen who were part of the diplomatic mission, received training in their duties. *Time to find out more about Amashi.* Diego decided the time was right to visit the teaching robot, Anaar. It was more than right—he felt a twinge of guilt that he hadn't seen Anaar earlier. With only a few days until the launch, he hoped he had enough time to learn everything he needed. He knew the main inhabitants were the sea dwelling Amashina. Diego needed to learn more if he planned on being a successful representative of the Empire.

"Rejas Anaar," Diego addressed the boxlike robot in the learning room. Anaar took charge in the boy's education when Ziron captured Diego and took him on board the ship. Whenever Diego had a question about something—and he had a lot of questions, even after all this time—he visited Anaar.

"Yes, Sub-Commander Diego Moon Crusher Perez," the robot answered in his low, pleasant voice.

"Santa Maria, you don't have to use my entire Seressin name. I haven't changed that much, have I?"

"Since coming on board, you have received two promotions and decorations and even had a name change."

"I am still Diego Perez, despite the long new name. Please, Rejas Anaar, just call me Diego."

"As you wish. Are you here to learn about the Amashi system and your role in the upcoming visit?"

"Yes, I should have come sooner, but I wanted to make sure our ship was ready."

"What we do not have time to go over before you leave, you can learn as you sleep."

"Good. Thank you."

"Let me show you a quick overview of the dominant life forms."

"Amashina, right?"

"Yes. Please watch."

Diego watched, still amazed at the way he could see a place far away by looking on a screen, which, in this case, was one side of Anaar's 'body.' The view was as though a starship approached from the outer reaches of the system. First, Diego observed a broken ring of small dwarf planets, along with fragmented chunks of rock. Next, the 'ship' approached an asteroid belt, then a small icy planet, the surface pitted and broken where objects had slammed into the lifeless orb. It had no atmosphere of note.

The next planet had an atmosphere, but a dry wind scoured one part of the planet, dumping the yellowish dust and dirt on another part. Diego figured Ziron would enjoy visiting that one better, even though it appeared beyond uninhabitable to him. The sky glowed yellow gray.

The next planet was bluish green, with thick, cottony bands of gold clouds circling the globe. From what Diego had learned from Anaar, Amashi had the same diameter as his home planet, Earth. The atmosphere contained higher amounts of oxygen and less nitrogen than Earth. They didn't need a respirator — he counted that as a plus.

However, any visitors required specialized equipment to visit with the Amashina. Diego had been told they would receive their equipment at the spaceport.

The approaching view took him through the clouds, thick with moisture, then toward the surface of the ocean. When the video slowed, Diego felt as though he was floating above the water toward a spot of land in the distance. That view slowed even more as the land drew closer. Twice, the video went through rain showers, once through low-lying clouds.

The Seressin had built the spaceport on an archipelago in the middle of the vast ocean. They had extended it so several spaceships could land simultaneously. One building loomed over the ocean, waves lapping against sturdy pilings. The video informed him this was the spaceport.

"This isn't the largest landform on the planet, but it is the most centrally located and the most stable."

"Stable? Are there earthquakes?" Diego asked.

Anaar continued. "In Amashi's southern hemisphere, they can be powerful. But the other factor is the weather. There are distinct seasons of storms. Winter storms lash the northern parts of the planet with ice, while in the equatorial areas, there are typhoons and hurricanes. You and your crew are arriving at the end of the second phase of storms. There might still be gales, but after the second weather phase, there is a lull in harsh weather."

"Good. One less thing to worry about," Diego murmured.

"During the first phase, the Amashina stay in the depths, not that they seem worried about it."

"They don't like the Seressin?"

"No, it's not that. The simple fact is that they are ambivalent to us."

"Can you tell me about them, Anaar?"

A new picture appeared on the robot's screen. It showed an animal somewhat resembling a dolphin, like the ones he had seen leaping beyond the surf when he visited Yerba Buena on a ship. They had fascinated him. These creatures equally fascinated him.

Anaar continued. "They communicate amongst themselves through clicking and clacking sounds that carry in the water. Some scientists believe they are also telepathic. Maybe the Turengen can tell since they have that ability."

"How can a diplomat communicate with them?" Diego asked.

"Through the use of individual implanted translators. These converse with visitors who wear similar communicators."

"And have to be implanted?" If so, Diego wondered just what he had gotten himself into.

"No, Diego, you wear yours."

Diego scratched behind his ear, puzzled. "I understand the idea of translating the clicks and clacks into Seressin, but how can I talk to them underwater? I will wear a helmet like when I have been in space. These are creatures limited to living in the water. Does an underwater helmet work the same way as a spacesuit helmet?"

"Yes. Visitors wear gear allowing for speech while swimming." Anaar showed him a picture.

The pictures were fascinating. "Oh. I have a lot to learn."

"Did you swim on your planet?"

Diego shook his head. "Only a bit of playing around in shallow lakes."

"This will be a fantastic learning experience for you, Sub-Commander Diego. A pleasant one. Oceans teem with life and have temperate waters.

Diego laughed. "As long as that life doesn't try eating me." Anaar didn't answer. "Tell me what I need to know to communicate with the Amashina so I don't insult them."

"Yes, and I can send you with a sleep disk to allow assimilation of the protocols on the way to Amashi."

Diego left the session grateful for Anaar's help. He pocketed the small disk. He didn't know how it worked, only that it did. Such a device had been invaluable when he had first come aboard *Star Devourer*.

CHAPTER THREE

Ziron scratched his cheek patch. "You have the greetings canister the Supreme Commander is sending to the Amashi leaders?"

"Yes, Marix."

"Good. And my salutations?"

"Yes, sir. It's in the same canister as Serix Marzor's communication."

"Excellent. I don't doubt you'll find this trip very entertaining and most educational," Ziron said.

"I hope so, Commander. And we will complete the mission with honor."

"I know you will, Sub-Commander. Go nobly and go with strength."

Diego ordered his crew into the commander's scout craft. He boarded last. Rrishan cycled the hatch closed behind him. Bress served as navigator and Rreengrol as the weaponry officer. Rrishan and Jeng were helmsmen, and Fress took care of communications. Despite being a small contingent, Diego was confident he had assembled a strong crew.

At his orders, the ship released the gravity anchors and lifted from the deck. The aft engines carried the ship out of the bay, and they soon streaked toward the nearest fold gate. As they were well into Seressin territory, there should be no enemy surprises, but Fress kept her eyes on the computer to detect anything out of the ordinary. Despite the fold gates, it would take a day and a half to get there.

Diego sent two of the Turengen and Rrishan to get something to eat and then sleep. He, Rreengrol, and Jeng took the first watch. This ship had a compact command station, allowing him to monitor all the ship's functions simultaneously. Diego realized that a year and a half ago, he knew nothing except ranching. He pulled his mind back to his duties.

When it came time for him to sleep, he wore the sleep learning device Anaar gave him. The soft sounds of Anaar's protocol instructions in his ears helped lull him to sleep. He woke up several hours later, feeling as though something had nudged him or called him, but he didn't remember any dreams.

The cabin's darkness told him it was too early for his shift. Diego checked his watch. Only four hours. So, what had awakened him? He lay back on the narrow bed, pressing the button for the lesson to resume. He couldn't recall falling back to sleep, but Bress shook him awake for his watch.

"Your turn," the Turengen mumbled, staring at him from the ladder.

One side of the cabin held the mounted bunk beds. Diego had chosen the top one. He slid off, glad the gravity was eighty percent normal for this ship. "Bress, next time call me if I'm not on duty when I should be."

"Will remember…"

Diego washed up, grabbed a first-meal tray, and headed toward the control room.

"Fine thing, the commander coming in late for duty," Rreengrol teased.

"Next time, wake me up when you get up!"

"As you command," Rreengrol replied, his grin still in place. "To be honest, I was half asleep when I crawled out of bed and didn't notice you still sleeping above me."

Diego nodded and sat in the command chair.

"What do you think Amashi will be like?" Diego asked as he bit into the protein first-meal bar.

"Very wet." Rrengrol laughed at his own joke.

"I have spent no time under the surface of the ocean. My

time on your world doesn't count."

"You haven't? I thought you said you lived not too far from an ocean," Rreengrol said.

Diego shook his head. "The land generated wealth. The ocean was only important because that's where the rain came from, and ships sailed in with supplies."

"We'll all learn then, won't we?"

"Yes." Diego gazed at the monitor while he munched on his breakfast. Distant stars moved at their different speeds. He checked the ship's systems and found everything to be working as they should. During their shift, he played Anaar's disk.

At the end of their duty, Diego grabbed a regular meal, heated it, and ate with Rreengrol and Fress. He tried to take a brief nap, but this time, sleep didn't come. Diego slid out of bed and worked out on the small exercise machine. Then he reviewed another of Anaar's disks. The little ship closed in on the gate to the Amashi system. Diego changed into his more formal uniform. When they passed through the gate, it wouldn't be long before they landed. Diego's anxiety rose again, and he wondered what had possessed him to volunteer for this.

He left Rreengrol and Fress sleeping and headed back to the control room. Bress jumped out of the command chair, but Diego waved him back. "It's still your watch, Bress. I'm only up here because I couldn't sleep. Have we gone through the gate yet? I didn't feel it." Diego sat in one of the navigational chairs.

"No, Commander, shortly. Twenty meka-drons."

"Good. We're not far. Carry on." Diego studied the procedure for their approach to the landing field on Amashi. *That's a landing field?* Just a small island with landing platforms built out over the reef. If the winds were capricious, which his information told him happened often, then landing could be tricky.

"Approaching fold gate, Commander," Bress called out.

Rreengrol and Fress strode into the control room.

"Entering the Amashi systemmmm," Bress's voice drawled out as they went through the fold gate. Diego felt the now-familiar stretching and then an immediate return to normalcy.

The ship's guidance system allowed them to make it through the small asteroid belt with only a few beeps of alarm. Those were small bits of debris the defensive shield incinerated. Diego watched Amashi growing larger in his monitor. They slid into orbit and awaited orders. After acknowledgment from the surface, the ship arrowed toward the ocean. The computers chirped coordinates and speed in a happy chorus.

As they descended through the clouds, turbulence buffeted them, but Bress never needed to take control from the computer. The forward thrusters slowed them and continued decelerating the ship until they were hovering over the island.

The ship touched down without incident. Before he unbuckled his safety harness, Diego gazed at the monitor, showing foamy waves breaking on the island's shoreline. The blue-green water soothed him, not much different from the ocean on his home world. Bress shut down the systems, secured the ship, and then they waited for the landing master's orders.

Before long, they were standing on the platform, breathing the salty air, as a robot greeted them. This one resembled a humanoid having a bulbous head on top of a triangular body. It had no legs, instead rolling and pivoting around on at least three wheels.

"Come with me, please," it said. "It is near evening. You will stay in the guest sleeping quarters tonight and meet with the Amashina first thing tomorrow in the morning."

Diego gripped the canister with diplomatic greetings under his arm, his small pack of personal effects on his back. The others followed him to an elevator, which took them to the next platform. When the door slid open, an amazing underwater scene greeted them.

As though reading his mind, the robot said, "We build guest quarters on the edge of the reef and underwater to make it easier for the Amashina to greet visitors. Follow me, please."

Diego paused as they walked past the large window showing off the Amashi world. Schools of fish flashed by the shadow of something that loomed nearby. Diego couldn't see the creature, but he saw plants or animals near the bottom change color — going from yellow to purple, red to orange, green to white. The shadow left, and the colors reverted to their original hues.

"Commander," Rreengrol quietly reminded him of the others.

"Oh. I'm sorry. That was fascinating." He fell behind the robot. Bress nudged his mind. Diego felt eager anticipation.

"The Amashina will direct excursions for any who desire to explore the ocean before the end of your mission," the robot said.

"Thank you. That sounds wonderful!"

They walked down a corridor with plush material on the walls and shiny deck material on the floor. That made sense, Diego thought, if one had water creatures walking the halls. The robot brought them to a desk where another machine sat.

The first robot wheeled backwards against the wall. "Our concierge will take care of your needs for tonight and then I will show you to your rooms."

"Please tell me your designations, names, and your species," the desk robot ordered.

"Species?" Diego asked, wondering the purpose for that.

"In order to meet the Amashina, you need to be outfitted for excursions into the ocean. We guarantee you have well-fitting suits with the right mix of breathing gasses."

"Oh. I am here for Commander Ziron of the Seressin

Empire. I am sub-Commander Diego Moon Crusher Perez, and I am human."

"Human? I have no listing for such a species."

Diego thought of the Latin term. "Homo Sapiens."

If such a creature could sigh, Diego swore the soft grinding was just that. "Commander, please wait. When we finish with the others, we will create a new listing for you." It gazed at him with glowing eyes. "From what planet did you arise?"

"Earth." Diego couldn't tell him more because the priest hadn't taught him astronomy. He didn't know how far from home he had traveled.

The robot had archived information for Grrlocks and Turengens. The first robot beckoned to them, and the second one addressed Diego. "Sir, I will take you to the measurement and cataloging center. You will meet with your crew in a short time."

"I will accompany Commander Perez," Bress stated, his short whiskers bristling.

"There is no need for that, Sub-Commander Bress. You can rest after your long trip here," the robot replied.

Bress folded his arms and repeated. "I will accompany my commander."

A few seconds of uncomfortable silence passed before the robot emitted the sighing, grinding sound.

"The rest of you relax in your rooms. Bress and I will join you as soon as I am cataloged," Diego said with a reassuring smile. Or what he thought resembled a reassuring smile. He didn't understand this paranoia on such a backwater and peaceful planet.

Rreengrol patted his belt, reminding Diego of the communicator each of them wore.

It seemed he wasn't the only paranoid member of their group. Diego gave a slight nod as the others followed the first robot.

Four more robots rushed around the measurement and cataloging room, overseen by a creature having similarities to a Turengen. It stood half again as tall as Bress, and its pelt looked like fuzzy fish-skin. The hands had three stubby fingers. It had no feet, only flippers reminding Diego of mermaid legends he had heard sailors tell when he visited the docks at San Pedro. Its large black eyes widened when he spied Diego, and he slid off his pedestal to approach.

It resembled a seal, Diego thought. It even barked like a seal.

"What are you?" the translator around its neck blared.

Diego repeated what he had told the robot.

"Your people have been here."

"No, A Seressin ship captured me. The people on my world have no knowledge of flying, spaceships, or even planets where other intelligent creatures live. I rode a horse to different places before Commander Ziron took me on board his ship."

The creature barked again. "You are sure of that?"

"I am positive. I'm Marix Ziron's sub-commander because I worked hard, and I have successfully completed several assignments he has given me." Diego then wondered at the seal-man's behavior. "Why did you say I had been here?"

"Because you look the same as the Old Enemy."

"Old Enemy?"

"Yes. They walked on two legs, had two arms, torsos like yours. Identical to you."

"In other words," Bress began. "Sapient bipeds."

"No, young Turengen. You have two legs, two arms, and a torso. You think, but you do not resemble your commander."

"I can't be one of these Old Enemies. It must be a coincidence."

"Yes," the seal barked. "It must be." But what came out of the translator didn't sound too sure.

Bress broke into Diego's thoughts. *Here comes another Amashi creature to check you out, Diego.*

Turning around, Diego spotted a creature walking on five tentacle-like hands. Each tentacle was the length of Diego's legs. Four took care of locomotion, and the fifth stuck out above its head like a snout testing the air. The head had eyes ringing the upper part of the cranium. Diego couldn't see a translator, but it wore one somewhere. Probably implanted, as Anaar had described.

"You resemble the descriptions of the Old Enemy," it said.

CHAPTER FOUR

"Can you tell me about this Old Enemy?" Diego asked. "I don't remember seeing a reference to it when I studied the information about your world."

The tentacle Amashina stated, "The Elder Leadership should be the ones to discuss the past with you. All I can say now is I am glad to see the Seressin giving greater roles to their non-Seressin members."

"To be honest with you, so am I. Are the elders those I am going to give greeting to tomorrow?"

One tentacle waved in the air. "Yes, they insisted they wanted to meet with you."

"Because I look like this Old Enemy?"

"I cannot say, sir."

"If my appearance will upset the Elders, my second in command can lead the mission here."

"No, no!" the creature said. "We don't believe you are a descendant of the Old Enemy, but the leaders cannot overlook the similarities."

I detect no deviousness in his thoughts, Diego. Only curiosity and a desire to learn. And to protect their interests.

"Very well. What do you want me to do now?" Diego glanced askance at the various machines and the robots attending them.

"We will take measurements of you. Our computers already contain the sizes and specifications for your companions, so they will rest while you are here. It will not take long. We need to make an underwater suit for you to travel safely in the Amashi world. We will also take readings on the gasses you need to sustain your life underwater and other factors regarding your health since you are an air breather."

Diego nodded, doubting they could do it in one night. The sea creatures and their robots used a variety of instruments to study the air he breathed, in and out. They took readings of the various parts inside his body, then measured his size and shape. While they were thorough, the robots were fast, too, and a robot led him to his room.

Entering the room, Diego noticed the others were in the middle of their meal. Engineers had designed and built their quarters underwater with an eating area and a view into the ocean, and there appeared to be doors into separate rooms. Bress confirmed the quarters contained individual bedrooms, six of them, although Diego knew the Turengens always slept together.

"How did everything go, Old Enemy," Rreengrol teased.

"Ha! Ha! I can't believe the wonders of science on other worlds. Things that beeped, chirped, squeaked, whirred, and whizzed diagrammed my body, inside and out," Diego said. He gazed at various dishes in the center of a table long enough for his entire crew. The bowls and plates were a light blue color, like turquoise, shot with gold sparkles dancing in the overhead lighting of the room.

The dishes were interesting enough, but as Diego sat, he studied the food. A fish, complete with fins and tail, stared back at him. Another bowl contained something with the consistency of porridge but was of a greenish color—very unappetizing to him. Bress passed him a bowl with what looked like a salad, but other than the stringy seaweed fronds, which were more brown than green, the other bits were unfamiliar.

"Delicious food, Commander," Bress commented. "Much better than ship's food."

"From what I have observed, anything tastes good to you!" Diego laughed as he took samples of everything except a vile greenish-yellow colored paste.

"That is sweet," Rrishan said, pointing to the paste. "Goes good on the toasted, whatever this is." She passed him the plate of what could be loosely called bread.

Diego admitted everything tasted good and matched any of the meals he had eaten on *Star Devourer*. When Diego finished, he studied the room. A meeting room lay next to the dining area, filled with large, comfortable chairs. Beyond that stood an immense window looking out into the sea. Diego strode over to the window. The sun had set, so little light shone from above, but somehow, plenty of light filtered in from the water itself.

Fish flitted or meandered along, most dotted with yellow lights, like little fireflies. Some lights flickered while others shone steadily. Growths glowed in various colors. A large shape resembling the hand-tentacle creature approached. It used its five legs to propel itself through the water while the eyes revolved around its head. It swam closer to the window, and Diego gasped at its size. He wondered how large the animals grew on Amashi.

An even larger shape darkened the water. It floated closer but never came near enough for Diego to see it. One long, silvery fin dangled past where he stood. It drew closer and then touched the window. Sparks along the fin danced at the contact. The creatures entranced Diego.

"I cannot wait to go swimming tomorrow," Bress said.

"Even with things that grow so big?" Diego teased.

Bress shrugged. "They are big for you, too."

"Yes, they are, but I don't think the Amashina would let off-world visitors go places where they could be in danger."

"Exactly, Commander."

Diego laughed. He had answered his own question. "I am eager, too."

"Tired. We are going to the sleep quarters now."

"Sleep well."

The Turengen trotted off to one room. The door slid open at their approach and closed behind them. Diego continued to peer out of the large portal.

Rrishan walked up beside him. "I can't wait either."

Rreengrol joined her. "I wonder about this Old Enemy business. Did they talk to you after we left?"

Diego shook his head. "They said the Amashina leaders wanted to talk to me about it tomorrow when they meet us."

Rrishan flicked her tail into the air. "Maybe these Old Enemies didn't have tails. Seressin have tails, Turengens, Breanths have tails. And, of course, Grrlocks have wonderful tails."

"Resh don't, but they aren't the Old Enemy the Amashina described." Diego smiled, and his reflection smiled back at him. "Well, they couldn't be people from my planet."

"From what you told me, I have to agree," Rrishan replied. She yawned, her sharp teeth glinting from her reflection. In an involuntary reaction, Rreengrol added his wide yawn.

"Let's head to our beds. A good night's sleep will make tomorrow more enjoyable," Diego said. "By the way, where do we take our dinner utensils and plates after we're finished?"

"Our server told me he and his companions would clean after we went to sleep," Rreengrol replied.

"Sounds good to me," Diego said. He remembered nothing after he pulled off his uniform and laid down.

CHAPTER FIVE

It amazed Diego when the seal-man arrived at their suite the next morning, six robots in tow, each carrying a package. The robots presented a package to every one of them, including Diego, with a suit allowing them to visit the ocean world. "How did you get this done so quickly?" The seamstresses on his father's hacienda took days, and Diego remembered the chastisement he received if he ripped or soiled his new clothes.

The creature ducked his head. "We use materials easy to work with, young commander. Many of our people are nocturnal, so they didn't mind directing the robots to have it prepared for your use this morning."

"Thank you," Diego said and then realized he had learned none of these being's names. "May I ask your name?"

"I am known as Skreelzix."

Despite the clicks and shrill elongations in the name, Diego attempted it. "Thank you, Skreelzix." He knew he butchered the name, but the Amashina didn't seem the least bit bothered.

"We will wait until you get into your suits. The helmets, gloves, and fins will be at the point of disembarkation."

Diego nodded and took his suit into his room. Removing his shipboard uniform, he touched the soft material before donning it. The clothing was extraordinary, bluish-black, and adorned with vivid yellow and red lines along the legs and arms. The material at the wrists, ankles, and neck was stiffer to attach the items Skreelzix mentioned. Although the suit stretched, it molded to his body. When he moved, the material acted like a second skin with no discomfort.

The fabric was thin, and Diego wondered how it could keep

him warm in what he presumed would be a cool environment. Diego noticed a patch of pumpkin-orange on the right side of his chest with nothing matching it on the left and wondered what its purpose was. He slid his hand along the sides of his body and shook his head at this amazing piece of technology. Diego pulled on his ship boots and left his other clothes in his pack.

When he left his room, the others were waiting. Diego blushed at the thought he spent so much time admiring a piece of clothing. He noticed their outfits were just as suited to his crewmates. The Turengens' suits accommodated their tails, which Diego knew they used when they swam. He didn't see Rreengrol and Rrishan's tails outside of their suits.

Rreengrol saw Diego looking. "We use our tails for balance, but not as much when swimming."

Every suit had bright spots and abstract designs on various parts of their arms and legs and different-colored patches on the chests. He would ask the Amashina what the symbols meant. The Turengen hadn't worn their footwear, but then Diego knew how comfortable the otter-people were in no clothing.

"Come," Skreelzix said. He and the robots led them out of the suite and down a corridor to an elevator. The elevator wasn't large enough to accommodate the Seressin contingent and the robots. "Remain until the elevator returns for you." The robots stopped and waited.

They entered the elevator and barely felt it moving. The doors opened into a large room with a pool. Diego realized it led to the ocean. Helmets, gloves, and footwear hung on racks nearby. In only a few minutes, the robots rolled out of the elevator and helped them find the rest of their equipment. One robot brought Diego a helmet and explained how to wear it. It was a perfect fit. He pulled it off. "Skreelzix, where does the air come from?"

"There is a mechanism in your helmet programmed to produce the exact blend of breathable gasses for each one of you from the water."

"Oh." Again, it amazed Diego. He put the helmet back on and took his gloves from the robot. The helmet weighed so little he could move his head with no restriction.

"Carry your footwear until you are ready to enter the ocean," Skreelzix instructed.

Diego's footwear resembled a large fish's fins.

The Turengen pattered over to the water with bare feet. Diego, only then, noticed the webbing between their toes. They also didn't have gloves. Bress held up one hand and spread his fingers, showing small webs of skin there, too. The Turengen had their helmets on, but he could hear their lively chattering through them.

He realized he heard them inside his helmet. "Are you talking to me, Bress?" Diego asked, dumbfounded. He tried turning on his communicator when another voice spoke.

"The communicator translates and allows you to connect with your crewmates to whom you wish to speak. It takes a bit of getting used to, but that is the best way we have of underwater speech among the varied species who visit Amashi. If one doesn't designate the person they wish to speak to, then the words will go out to those nearby," Skreelzix explained. "You will hear the words of the Amashina Elders when they speak to you, as well."

"How handy," Rreengrol murmured. "We need these on the ship."

Diego smiled. He couldn't imagine someone talking to one person and everyone else hearing the exchange.

Skreelzix dismissed all but one robot. "It won't be long before we go to meet the leadership."

"Thank you," Diego said, handing the canister with Ziron's greetings to Skreelzix. "They assured me this is waterproof."

The seal-man studied it with his flipper-hands and handed it back. "It will withstand the pressures of the swim to our elders, but if it doesn't, you can convey the greetings yourself."

Diego swallowed. Somehow, that didn't make him feel confident.

CHAPTER SIX

A tentacled Amashina swam up to the edge of the water and then 'walked' the rest of the way out. "The Elder Leaders are waiting to speak to you, Commander. Your crew members will be in attendance as well. Follow me, but before you do so, please put on your flippers."

"We do not need ours, sir," Fress said. She lifted her foot and showed the usually unseen leathery webs.

The creature waved one tentacle. "We made your footwear optional, young Turengen."

During this exchange, Diego sat down and pulled on his fins, which were shaped like Skreelzix's flippers. He hoped it wouldn't take him long to get used to them. He stood back up at the edge of the water and tried to lift his foot, but he felt off balance.

"Just walk into the water, Commander," the Amashina coaxed.

Diego shuffled forward, not wishing to fall face-first. He walked down a ramp, but as the water came up to his knees, then his waist, it pushed against him like gentle breezes blowing in every direction. Suddenly, there was no bottom, and his body dropped into the ocean. He held his breath.

He heard a voice inside his helmet. "Breathe normally, Commander."

Diego hesitated but finally took a shallow breath, then another. The helmet somehow gave him air, and unlike the suits he wore to work outside the spaceship, he couldn't even hear the soft whooshing of the air. "This is amazing!" Diego forgot to watch for the ground and almost lost his balance when his feet touched the sand of the ocean floor.

"Come toward me, Commander," a soothing voice in his head instructed.

Several tentacles motioned to him, and Diego knew this was his instructor. He started out trying to walk, but his flippers caught in the sand, and he fell forward. Then Diego employed movements he used back home when he ventured into the ocean. He moved his arms to sweep the water back and paddled his feet. With ridiculous ease, Diego swam forward. He back-pedaled to avoid the Amashina. He needn't have worried. The tentacle-hand creature moved out of his way with graceful ease.

Diego stopped and gazed around. Near his feet, he spied tiny plants with flowers waving in the currents of the water. The blossoms were bright yellow, and the rest of the plant red. Looking farther, Diego found the entire area carpeted with plants in a variety of hues and sizes. "Skreelzix, what kind of plants are these?" he asked, pointing.

"They are not plants, nor are they animals. They are a type of in-between creature."

Before Diego could speak, a Turengen swam past him, circling and twisting around the Amashina. Two others dashed by his head, streaking to the surface and back again.

Bress's chittering sounded in his ears. "This is fun. I like this place."

Diego swam with hesitation at first, getting better used to the fins and his suit. He noticed the gloves also had webbing. No wonder he almost ran into the Amashina. After a while, Diego comfortably swam in any direction. He studied an outcropping of rocks covered with different colored growths. These reminded him of lichens he sometimes saw on oak trees. Another plant — or animal — was large and spiny, resembling a ferocious sagebrush.

Rreengrol and Rrishan swam near him. The younger Grrlock swam ahead, trying to follow the lead of the Turengens, but despite her agility, she couldn't keep up with them. They continued to twist, spiral, and dive toward the bottom or the surface.

"Are the suits satisfactory?" An unfamiliar voice — one deep and rumbling — spoke to him.

Diego looked around and noticed a creature having the general shape of a dolphin, but its front flippers were longer and ended in stubby fingers. An Amashina leader. He recognized it from his studies on the *Star Devourer*. It resembled dolphins he had once seen in California. This one also had an up-curved mouth, making it look as though it smiled at him. The tail was larger, but the eyes mesmerized him. They contained a pinpoint of black in the middle, but the rest of the eye resembled burnished gold radiating outward, like a sunburst.

"Come, Commander Diego Treshtura-lun Perez. You and your crew are expected. Have you mastered your suits and the art of swimming in our world?"

"Yes, thank you. The suits are amazing."

"We made them to compensate for pressure changes, provide breath, and warmth."

"I appreciate your people making them for us." Diego paused. "How do I address you?"

"I am Frake, an aide to our Elder Leaders. I will guide you to the meeting place and anywhere else you go while on our world. We are happy to have you and your group representing the Seressin Empire."

Diego wondered again about the Old Enemy but figured they would explain everything when they met. "Shall we go, then?"

"Yes, come. Stay near me for safety, although there should be little harm. We will go into deeper waters, but your suits will compensate for all factors except a violent attack. Please let me know if you experience any problems."

"We will, Frake." Diego couldn't keep his eyes off everything he saw on their way into the deeper waters. He noticed the sand glinted like silver or bronze where the sun filtered through the water. Little shelled crabs scuttled along the bottom, except these were flat, like tiny dinner plates with their legs hidden under round, flat shells. Tiny heads with flaring antennae stuck out of the front of the animals. He noticed starfish, except these had long, spidery legs, lots of them. They scuttled for a short distance and then shot into the water like rockets.

Frake matched their speed as they swam into the deeper realm of the Amashi Ocean. Diego hoped they could explore when the official business concluded. As they descended, the light dimmed, but a glow from creatures swimming alongside them, as well as luminescent creatures attached to rocks, compensated. Blue dominated, but he noticed many other colors.

Diego studied Frake and wondered how he spoke to them. While his mouth opened and closed, Diego only picked up clicks and squeaks. The voice he heard in his helmet modulated with a computer quality, but better.

The communicator in our suits translates Frake's language into Seressin for us, Bress explained. *I believe they are also somewhat telepathic.*

The group swam through a tunnel lit with more of the luminescent growths. He noticed the lights dimming and brightening in patterns—blue, then yellow, green, then gold, and all over again. Diego believed it was a greeting from the Amashina leadership. It reminded him of the dancers back in the pueblo who communicated with their fans.

CHAPTER-SEVEN

"Welcome to the Leadership Hall, Commander Diego Treshtura-lun Perez," Frake said.

Diego made no comments as they continued. First, they swam through a short tunnel and into a chamber breathtaking in simplicity but elegant. He noticed rocks shaped like smooth, translucent rods rising from the floor, some to a height Diego couldn't determine. The rods contained colors resembling the patterned lights that led them inside. Silver rods were the brightest, overwhelmingly bright, but golden-yellow rods dimmed and brightened in a soothing cadence.

The ocean floor appeared to be cultivated with flower-like creatures in clusters of similar sizes, colors, and shapes. The ocean current flowed gently in this area, but the creatures still waved back and forth in unison. Diego thought it a relaxing way to begin a meeting.

The silver rods dimmed, and Diego could see the four Amashina waiting at the end of the chamber. They resembled Frake, only they appeared to be older. How he knew, Diego couldn't tell. They looked the same, with the same rubbery, smooth skin. As they drew closer, these Amashina not only appeared older but larger. One of them was a deeper gray than the others. Diego touched the canister he had secured to the belt around his waist.

"Welcome, Commander Diego Treshtura-lun Perez," a lyrical higher-pitched voice sounded in his helmet. "And welcome to your very diverse crew. It is indeed an honor to have you here."

"The honor is ours, Excellency."

He heard soft laughter. "Excellency? We are of higher experience and knowledge than the rest of our kind, but none of us are excellent."

"My training didn't educate me on the greeting I should give to the Leadership of Amashi, so I chose what I thought was best from my experience."

"How very flattering, Commander. We use very few honorifics here on Amashi. Usually, we go by our names. Mine is Feelona." She raised her flipper/hand.

Diego bowed the best he could in the water. It was more of a nod.

"I am Flash," a deep-voiced male next to Feelona said with a slight bow of his body. He didn't appear capable of such a gesture, but it looked graceful. Diego returned the bow.

"I am Falosh," another deep-voiced Amashina said — the third from the right.

"I am F'shon," the last one, a female, said.

Diego bowed again. His crew did the same. "I have greetings from my Marix, Commander Ziron."

"Please convey the greetings to us. While we could make out the glyphs eventually, we know you are aware of your commander's words."

Feelona served as the spokesperson of the group. Diego dug into his mind for Ziron's sentiments, trying to remember the words verbatim.

The diplomatic document is waterproof, Commander, Bress reminded him.

Feeling an embarrassed flush creep up his cheeks, Diego unscrewed the canister and pulled out the contents. He paraphrased Commander Ziron's salutations. "The commander sends you his greetings from the Serix of the Seressin Empire, who wishes you long life and prosperity. Ziron sent us to convey his friendship and cooperation." Diego put the message back in the canister and unclipped it from his waist. "Do you wish to keep the document? Or send back a message?"

"Commander Diego, please tell your Marix Ziron we appreciate his and his Serix's heartfelt greetings and good wishes. We hope the same fortune for him."

"We appreciate your hospitality and hope all is well on your world."

"Again, thank you. Our people are prospering."

Diego considered this part of the meeting fluffy formality, like a formal dance he once observed at his father's hacienda. He didn't have to wait long for confirmation.

"If you have time for informal discussions, we would appreciate it. Then you and your crew can enjoy the beauties of our world. Let's swim to a protected meeting place where nothing will disturb us."

Diego nodded. "Of course, Feelona."

"Please, follow us. It is not a long trip."

The leadership led them through a much narrower tunnel. Frake followed behind them. Everything became more somber.

CHAPTER EIGHT

Diego noted his surroundings but didn't study them this time. He sensed an urgency in the Amashina and concentrated on swimming as efficiently as he could. Fress and the other Turengen swam just ahead. Rreengrol and Rrishan swam on either side of him as they descended. Just enough light-giving creatures grew in the tunnel for them to see their immediate surroundings, but soon, the shadows deepened and grew spooky.

The Amashina slowed as Diego's legs and side burned from swimming.

"We are approaching a secure meeting place now. We enter slowly."

That is Falosh. The way ahead looked narrow, so Diego paused for Rrishan to swim ahead. Rreengrol fell behind. The Turengen swam ahead and soon faded into the dark tunnel. A small streak of bright yellowish-green light shone on one side. It was a long worm clinging to the rock wall, one longer than he had ever seen. When Diego swam closer, he confirmed it. They continued through the tunnel until they entered a small cavern.

The walls were plain, but a thin layer of flowery creatures covered the floor. The dim light muted their bright colors.

"Please, make yourselves comfortable on the floor," Falosh instructed.

"It won't hurt them?"

"No."

Diego kept his arms and legs still, and he sank to the bottom of the cavern, making himself as comfortable as he could.

"We need to tell you our history so you can understand the shock of our greeters yesterday." F'shon, the darker Amashina, spoke. "We began believing the Old Enemy tales were just that—tales. Something embellished from a tiny kernel of fact."

"But now we see there are beings resembling the Old Enemy of the tales," Feelona added.

"Do you believe I am one of these beings?"

Feelona opened her mouth in what Diego believed was a toothy smile. "We believe what you have told us, but if these beings should decide to return...."

"The history," F'shon reminded her colleagues.

"I am interested in hearing your history," Diego said.

"Many eons ago, land areas made up a larger proportion of the planet, with ten percent being composed of land. That land lay just north of the spaceport. There were creatures there that ate open-air vegetation growing in the ground. We of the oceans lived and died in our pods or communities, only killing to eat, never in anger or a desire for power. We assumed the land creatures did the same."

Feelona continued. "We didn't communicate with other species as we do today, but we had alliances among ourselves. Then, a ship landed. After that, more landed. Our people watched from just below the surface and saw creatures similar to you, Commander, as they exited their ships and explored the land areas. They checked the water; they checked the air. A large group of them started building places to live using things they pulled from their ships. They also cut the trees and used rocks. After there were enough buildings, the remaining spaceship left. Sometimes other ships came, but they didn't stay."

F'shon took up the narrative. "As the years passed, the buildings grew more numerous. They covered the above-ground land. The land-dwellers built ships to cross the ocean. Some sank during storms. We examined them." F'shon paused. "We get storms, but since most of us can avoid them underwater, we didn't consider them more than a nuisance."

"Still, these people began hunting us in the waters, using large vessels to find, kill, and drag our ancestors' bodies onto their ships. We assumed they used our people for food." F'shon's voice seemed to lower to almost a whisper. "Some of the undersea people disappeared — became extinct because of this hunting. As the air-breathing people became more numerous, they hunted us even more. They began fighting among themselves. Then, one day, the History says, it was like another sun shone overhead, exploding above the homes of the alien people. It destroyed the land people. Most of the land disappeared. This incredible destruction wiped many of our people out. Only those of us who lived on the other side of Amashi survived — at least, that's what the History said. The sun remained dark for many days, and the waters in this hemisphere grew cold and desolate. Those who did this were labeled as the Enemy. After even more time passed, we called them the Old Enemy."

"We are afraid of these beings returning with the power to destroy as the Old Enemy did," Feelona added.

"You don't have to worry about my people. They can't even fly in space. The Seressin have such weapons, but you are not at war with them," Diego explained, picking his words carefully.

"We feared when Seressin, in their ships, landed. We watched them, afraid of what they might do to us, despite not looking like the enemy of the long-ago time. Then they came near the water and communicated with us. They told us our planet was part of their empire. The Seressin told us they planned to build a landing place for their ships," Flash said. "They leave us alone most of the time. We have small trade agreements, but we need nothing from anyone off planet. The Seressin have honored their promises and have hunted none of our people. The Seressin don't care for our world. It's too wet for them."

Diego couldn't help it; he smiled. "That was the reason we

came instead of Marix Ziron."

"Still, the fact these creatures came in a spaceship, disgorged their people, and then left disturbs us, even after all these eons of time. The ones here destroyed themselves, but what about those on their home planet? What if they come back?" Feelona asked.

Diego thought for a few moments. The Seressin told him he was unique among their subjects, although they were familiar with mammalian creatures. So, the Seressin didn't know these Old Enemies. This information was something Commander Ziron would want to know. "Do you mind if I convey this to my commander, Marix Ziron?"

"We would appreciate it if you didn't. Our reaction yesterday compelled us to explain. Otherwise, you would have many questions and would not trust us."

"I understand, and as long as this doesn't obstruct Seressin security, I will honor your request."

CHAPTER NINE

"In the meantime, do you want to explore our oceans?" Feelona asked.

"Yes, but I am curious about something," Diego ventured.

"Yes?" Feelona asked.

"Why did we come here to discuss this?" To Diego, it seemed over-dramatic.

Feelona swam closer. "We have pod-members who would object to discussing our history with anyone from off-planet."

"I understand," he said, even though he didn't.

"Since we are already at this depth, would you like to explore nearby before returning to the upper levels?" Falosh asked. "Frake and Flash can escort you."

"Wonderful! And if any of my crew would prefer to rest, can they return with you?"

"Of course, Commander."

Diego turned to the rest of his delegation, but they all opted to stay and swim.

"We will see you after the sun sets, Commander Diego," Feelona said as the three Amashina disappeared.

"Where did they go?" Rreengrol asked, surprised.

"They have their own way, young Commander," Flash replied. "Come, let's explore. We rarely have anyone come this deep, so few have seen the many wonders on this level."

"How long can we breathe in these suits?" Diego asked.

"Indefinitely, in theory," Frake answered. "But we will go toward the surface before the sun sets."

The Turengens cavorted through the water as Diego and the Grrlocks swam through the tunnel. Flash was correct about the wonders in these depths, and Diego strained to see each living creature.

Flash led the group, and Frake took up the rear. Diego studied the technique of Amashina swimming. The large flukes propelled Flash forward with a minimum of effort. The fins acted as a rudder.

As they continued, fewer of the light creatures clung to the walls.

Flash swam beside him. "You have a pocket at your side where you will find a hand light to help you see in the depths."

Diego found the pocket and pulled out a rod. It was smooth with no buttons or switches, but when he reached for it, the device glowed, shining a wide light toward the ocean floor beneath them. Small animals skittered out of the way while those attached to the rocks waved fronds, strands, or flowers as far back from the light as they could. In the distance, small buttons of various colored lights winked on and off. "What are those?"

"They are other citizens of the ocean out hunting," Frake replied.

Diego sensed something. Other creature's thoughts—not Turengen—nibbled at his mind.

You are correct, Commander.

Diego decided not to respond. Bress could observe them and would warn him. They continued downward. His ears popped a time or two, but everything else worked normally.

"My ears hurt," Rrishan said.

"If you swallow a few times, you should be able to equalize the pressure," Flash told her. "We will adjust your suits tonight so it doesn't happen again."

Farther ahead, Diego's light picked out something that resembled a cultivated field. Rows and rows of life forms grew, their short fronds waving from side to side. Diego swam closer.

Frake swam in front of him. "We cultivate these in the

depths because they grow better in darkness."

"Oh, so it is a field. Intriguing!" They swam beyond the 'field' and into an area of craggy rocks and more sparse growth. Diego shined his light into the dark crevices. He spied small eyes staring at him before they jerked away. Farther on, he saw what they were. They reminded him of snakes, but these underwater creatures had several rows of sharp teeth and bright red skin.

"Don't get too close. Their bites are poisonous," Flash warned.

They continued swimming, finding new creatures everywhere they looked. Bress, Jeng, and Fress darted around, gyrating through the water, chasing each other, and scooting between rocks and waving creatures. This was something they hadn't been able to enjoy for quite some time.

Rrishan found a small sack in her pocket and used it to hold a shell she discovered. She looked up at Frake and asked, "Is it permitted?"

Frake smiled. "You are more than welcome, as long as it isn't attached to anything. At the end of your stay here, we will inform you if you have something that cannot leave Amashi."

"Thanks." She swam farther away, examining everything under her light.

Diego swam behind her. His ears popped, and he heard a soft rumbling. The ground danced in the light of his rod. Debris fell in a weird slow-motion dance from nearby crags; a few at first, then more rocks, sand, and dead creatures. The water buffeted him, sand billowed up, and the Turengen swam closer.

"A seaquake," Frake called out. "Come back toward me!"

The rumbling grew louder. Then, a squall rang in his ears. The buffeting eased up, and the rocks stopped rolling down the underwater slopes.

CHAPTER TEN

"Rreengrol?" Diego called out.

"Yes, I am alright."

"Bress?"

"Fine. Jeng and Fress are as well."

"Rrishan?"

Diego heard no answer.

I don't hear her, Fress said.

"Rrishan!" Rreengrol called out. They still received no answer. "We have to find her!"

"She was ahead of me." Diego pointed as he swam, his light barely piercing the churned-up water.

Rreengrol kept right beside him. "Rrishan!"

Diego stopped before a wall of rocks. Silt still drifted into the darkness below them. "The rocks covered her!" He dug furiously. The Turengen, Rreengrol, and the Amashina joined him. His crewmembers weren't as careful as the dolphin people and slung the rocks in a pile. Finally, they saw Rrishan's leg.

Rreengrol pulled off rocks at a furious pace until he uncovered his sister.

Diego's eyes zeroed in on the slow rise and fall of her chest. "She's unconscious but alive."

Rreengrol checked his sister. "I examined my sister's suit and found no damage, but I suspect her arm might be broken."

"Let me carry her. I have more strength," Flash told them. "We cannot rush to the surface. Your suits, while they adapt well to changes in pressure, must have time to do so."

Flash scooped Rrishan up and swam at a leisurely rate toward the surface. Rreengrol swam right next to him. Diego looked around and saw Rishan's sack. He picked it up and tied it to his belt. Then he followed. His monitors registered an aftershock, and a few rocks tumbled to the ocean floor. Diego caught up with the others.

When they reached the surface, several of the robots were waiting with a wheeled litter. Before a robot could take Rrishan, Rreengrol gathered her into his arms, kicked off his flippers, and carried her to the litter.

"They will transport her to the med bay where the medical robots will take care of her," Frake explained.

"I'm going too," Rreengrol growled, jerking off his helmet.

"As commander of this mission, I should attend to my injured crewmember," Diego stated, pulling off his flippers, then his helmet.

"I am sorry this happened. These quakes have been prevalent in recent days, but never this strong," Flash explained. "I must report to the leadership."

Diego nodded as the robots pushed the cart away from the water. A slight tremor rippled under his feet.

In the med bay, Diego watched as the medical robot checked Rrishan, then eased off her suit, careful of her arm. He saw machines like those used on him on the *Star Devourer* and knew she was in expert hands. "Rreengrol, I am going to visit the leadership. There's something going on that doesn't seem right. You stay here and report your sister's status when they tell you something."

Diego saw Fress watching from just inside the door. "You can send Fress with any information."

"Thanks."

Diego left the med bay, returning to the ocean entrance. Bress and Jeng were still there, as was a robot. "Where is the leadership?" he asked the robot.

"They are in the ocean meeting place."

"Which one? The one nearby or the more secure place?"

"Nearby, Commander."

"Thank you." He turned to the Turengen. "We're going for a swim. You remember how we got to the first meeting place?"

"Yes, Commander," Bress and Jeng said simultaneously.

Diego pulled on his flippers and helmet and walked into the ocean. "Take Commander Rreengrol's equipment to our room, please," he addressed the robot.

"Yes, sir."

Diego followed the Turengen, feeling more comfortable in his swimming skills as they made their way through the shadowy water. It didn't seem as long to reach the undersea grotto this time; they did no sightseeing. As the robot said, most of the leadership had gathered in the larger cavern, including Flash, Feelona, and Falosh. The fourth Amashina was absent.

"We were expecting you," Feelona said. "I am sorry concerning the injury to your crewmember. However, our medical facilities are excellent. She should recover completely."

"I get the impression these seaquakes have surprised you as much as they surprised us. Can I assume you rarely have these kinds of problems?"

The Amashina glanced at each other. Feelona said, "No, they are a recent occurrence. We are studying the problem. This is an old planet, Commander, and the ocean floors have been stable for many generations."

Diego sighed. "I am not a scientist, Leader. In fact, a year and a half ago, I would have understood none of this. My home planet is rather primitive, but I have felt earthquakes and have heard some of my people, the grandparents, talk about earthquakes they have experienced. Now that I know more science, I can't imagine the ground would just decide to shake without a reason."

"You understand a great deal," Falosh said. "We suspect

these occurrences are not natural, especially since they are happening where the Old Enemy used to live. Our technology says seaquakes should not be occurring here."

"Do you have an idea...?" Diego had trouble thinking of the scientific word.

Epicenter.

"Where the epicenter is?" *Thanks, Bress.*

"Yes, our technology robots got a clearer picture with this latest quake."

"I think a group of us should check out the area. See if something is causing these quakes," Diego suggested, paranoia creeping into his thoughts.

"We will consider this. And you wish to be included?"

"At least me and the Turengen. Rreengrol will stay with his sister. The Turengen are very savvy with the scientific instruments we have on our ship."

"Of course. And the eyes of those who do not live here may see something we miss."

Diego nodded his agreement.

"You and your crew should rest, and then we can go out in the morning."

This time, Diego shook his head. "I think we need to go during the nighttime when we have the cover of darkness. Even though it's dark down there anyway, I think this is the best time to check out the epicenter."

"Are humans always this impatient?" Feelona asked, her tone one of curiosity, not derision.

Diego felt warmth rise to his cheeks. He remembered coyotes usually hunted during the night. Bandits struck at night when their quarry grew less attentive. The cover of darkness made it easier to hide. He mentioned this to the Amashina.

"Your arguments would be logical if we were dealing with something on land, but the place where we are going is deeper, where the sun doesn't penetrate. It is dark all the time. Most sentient beings need a rest. Is that not true for humans?"

Now Diego felt embarrassed. "I spoke out of ignorance, Leader."

"No, you spoke out of concern. We will compromise. You and your crew rest until before sunrise and then meet back here. We will begin our journey before daylight because your arguments are sound."

Diego bowed to the leaders—at least as much as he could in the water. "We will return here before dawn."

They swam back to the sleeping quarters, where Diego headed to the medical facility. Rreengrol sat in the outer waiting room, his chin on his chest. Before Diego could reach out and make him aware of his presence, the Grrlock jerked up and gazed at him.

"How is she?" Diego asked.

"Rrishan is still unconscious. The robot said she had a concussion and a broken arm. It said she would be fine with rest. I'm waiting for her to awaken." He paused, then sucked in a deep breath. "I'm responsible for her."

"Rrishan joined the crew, knowing the risks. She desired to be a squire like you. Your sister joined because she wanted to be her own person. You have duties, too, so you can't be her babysitter, and she wouldn't want you to be. But this time, being here with her is the right thing." He sat with Rreengrol, saying nothing for a few minutes. "We are going out with a party of Amashina before dawn."

"Then you need to rest. I can join you after she awakens."

"Alright. I just wanted to see how you and Rrishan were doing."

"Thanks, my friend. And good luck in the morning."

Diego nodded and headed back to the room. Bress waited just inside the door. "She will be alright."

"Yes. She will." Diego changed the subject. "So, the Amashina feel there are intruders on the ocean floor?"

Bress made a slight chirring noise in his throat. "Feelona does. The others aren't so sure. Feelona thinks the Old Enemy has returned."

"Which may explain why they reacted the way they did when I arrived."

Bress chittered a laugh. "You startled them. You fit their memories of this ancient enemy."

"Let's rest." In his room, Diego did nothing but take off his underwater suit and shoes and then lay on his bed. He thought about what Feelona said, grateful they hadn't thrown him back on his ship and shipped him off-planet.

CHAPTER ELEVEN

Diego strode down a corridor in his underwater suit, his flippers in one hand. Water formed the walls, and he shuddered to think it could collapse on him. His helmet was unlocked, so he fastened it. Mist curled around his feet, that splashed in about two inches of cold, dark water.

A light shone ahead of him — a glow that didn't get brighter. Was someone walking away? Diego dug in his pocket for the Amashina glow stick. He found one and pushed the little button. Nothing happened. Diego tried again. Still nothing. As he looked up, he noticed the tunnel had shrunk. The water walls were closer, and he saw various sea creatures swirling around and trying to push through into the corridor.

Diego ran toward the light, ignoring the rocks and pebbles beneath his feet. The tunnel grew even smaller. With a roar, the water collapsed behind him, and he could feel the air pushing him forward. The light grew larger. As the water overtook him, Diego saw several creatures resembling him, even though their hair and eyes were a different color. One of them beckoned to him, and Diego pulled himself to his feet, reaching out for the person's outstretched hand.

They touched, and Diego found himself inside a ship or some kind of metal container. He was dry, the other person was dry. There was no wall of water, no sea creatures. Diego stared around and saw a building resembling a castle. "I am a Trolog. Come with me, Diego Perez. We will explore Trologar together." This was the person who had reached out to him. Diego followed her into the castle.

Something buzzed in his ear, and Diego jerked up, gasping. A dream. Had he seen the Old Enemies? He shook his head to clear his mind. This was the most confusing dream he had yet experienced. Throwing on his clothes, Diego met the Turengens out in the common area.

"Rreengrol is in his room. Rrishan must have awakened and is all right."

"Good!"

It didn't take them long to reach the ocean access and then the cavern. Flash waited for them. Without comment, they swam to the upper-level cavern where they met the previous day. Feelona and the other Amashina were there. The colored stripes were subdued, as were the light spots on the walls.

"So, you believe there is intelligence behind this?" Feelona asked when they all arrived.

"I don't know what to think, but I want to consider and discard even the strangest theory, as I believe you do." Diego wondered about his dream. How could these Old Enemies start an earthquake? He knew back on Earth, people once believed devils caused earthquakes, but that wasn't the case here. Diego remembered that Seressin technology had caused the destruction of a whole moon, so why couldn't a man-made device cause Amashi seaquakes? They needed to find out and stop it if these enemies had returned — Trologs? Diego remembered the name from his dream.

"We need to find the epicenter soon," Diego insisted.

"Very well, Frake, Flash, Falosh, and several deep-water Amashina will accompany you and your crew," Feelona said.

Flash wore an object encircling one of his fins. It flashed every few seconds with a deep blue light. The Amashina saw him gazing at it. "This device tells us where the seaquakes are coming from when they happen."

A creature reminding Diego of one of the enormous whales on his home world hovered near his head. "We are the teeloss Amashina. The deep-water kin," came a wavery, soft voice in the earpiece of his helmet. Various types of barnacle-type creatures crusted the long snout. Like the other Amashina, the fins ended with several long fingers. It swam past him and stopped in front of Feelona.

After what Diego assumed was a conversation, it swam back to Diego and the Turengens. "So, you are not the Old Enemy," it whispered.

"I am not your enemy," Diego replied.

"If we are to work together, I need to taste you."

"What!"

CHAPTER TWELVE

"I taste the water currents flowing past you and the water currents flowing through you." It drew closer.

Diego could see the Teeloss was twice his size—about a dozen feet long.

Commander, I believe she means to feel the currents of your thoughts. To understand how you think, Bress reassured him.

"Oh. Very well. So, it only involves you picking up my thoughts?"

"Indeed. And your inner currents," the Teeloss said. "Just stay still."

Diego did, and something tickled his mind. It differed from Bress and his people. He heard soft music, a chant of some sort. It reminded him of the clattering of crabs, the whoosh of the waves, and the drifting sands on the ocean floor. It went through his body and conjured up scenes from his home world—the sun, the hills, the horses, and cattle. Then it drifted away, and Diego blinked, gazing at the miniature whale.

"Definitely not an enemy." It swam toward the Turengen and repeated its actions. No, *her* actions. Even as she 'tasted' the Turengen, two other Teeloss came into the cavern and swam close.

The interaction was brief, a slight tickle of the brain before they moved on. "Do you have names?" Diego asked.

"Names? We know each other by our currents. Did you not feel a difference?" the first one asked, swimming back.

"No, except for the fact your two friends 'tasted' me for a much shorter time." Diego heard a wavery laugh.

"Then perhaps I am long, and they are short."

"Both of them?"

"Short Old," Fress suggested. "And Short Young."

Diego frowned. "Too complicated. How about Short and Elder?" He reached his hand out and touched the one he supposed to be the oldest on the snout. More growths covered her body. "Elder?"

"Yes."

He glanced at the other one. He looked shorter. "Short."

"Yes, Commander from Far Away. We should go now that we have names," Long said with a lilt of humor in his mental voice.

"I think so." Diego didn't know who the leader was, but Flash, Frake, and Falosh deferred to the three Teeloss. The whale people swam out of the cavern. He and the Turengens followed with the Amashina at the end. Once they were in the open, the Teeloss moved more freely, swimming close, then farther away, circling and almost dancing with each other. It fascinated him, but Diego wasn't interested in any time-wasting activities. Then he realized that what appeared as haphazard swimming didn't slow the group. The Teeloss kept their pace slower for him. *He* was the slow one. Diego's face flushed with embarrassment, but knew they couldn't see it. He continued his steady strokes.

He and the otter people didn't use their lights. The Teeloss had glowing lines the length of their bodies, as did the Amashina. Diego and his group followed the light of their guides. They continued downward, but Diego experienced no discomfort from increased pressure. He wondered at the abilities of those limited to living in the ocean — how they could make suits, create robots, and build spaceports. He would have to ask when they finished this assignment.

The ocean grew darker, with only the glow of various creatures' lights keeping him from feeling someone had tossed him into a pit. Little pinpricks of illumination came and went like the fireflies back home. Only these were different colors.

Diego could see little bits of light below him.

One of the Amashina said, "We are at the ocean floor. Swim more slowly so we can detect where these seaquakes are coming from," Flash said. "I will go ahead."

"What if there are no seaquakes while we are here?" Diego asked.

"I am getting a few readings from the last quake, so perhaps we will find out what we need to know without another seaquake."

Diego watched Flash. The Amashina swam a hundred feet and then stopped, waiting for more signals. Bress, Jeng, and Fress stayed close.

I am feeling something in my mind. Something not of this group, Bress thought.

Diego felt a pang of anxiety. Who else could be here? A different group of Amashina? *Do you know where it's coming from?*

Deeper, farther ahead. Cannot tell what kind of creature. Only a touch here and there.

Bress's thoughts troubled him, and Diego remembered his dream and felt anxiety welling.

Flash swam ahead, and the group followed. Everyone stayed closer together. Again, only the glowing lights on various creatures broke the deep darkness seeping inside his mind. Flash stopped again.

Bress tapped Diego's sleeve and pointed into the darkness ahead of them. He spied fewer creatures using the lights.

"The small ones are feeling something ahead?" Elder asked.

"Yes," Bress answered. "There is more down there than just shifting and shaking rocks."

As though on cue, the ground trembled, then shook harder and harder. A shriek sounded in Diego's helmet. He wanted to cover his ears but couldn't. It didn't come from a creature; it came from the ocean floor itself. Fist-sized rocks pummeled him, and he swam forward. "This way," he called when he reached a place where falling debris didn't reach them. He struggled to make out Bress and Jeng. "Fress?"

This is the right way. Fewer rocks. Bress swam ahead.

Fress swam up and leaned against his side.

CHAPTER THIRTEEN

Diego glanced around to see where the Amashina were, but the darkness was almost complete. The ground continued to rumble and shake. Bress led them downward. Diego trusted him and followed without comment, not wanting to give themselves away communicating through the helmets. The shaking eased.

Finally, Bress stopped and pointed to a large outcropping of rocks. Beyond them, he saw several lights, but these weren't from creatures. Three round, equal-sized lights glowed on the ocean floor. It was a machine—a sort of ship. If the lights hadn't been on, it would have been impossible to see. Diego suspected sentient beings were in the machine. He wondered if they had weapons.

Bress pointed and then swam away. Diego and the other Turengen followed. The otter-man led them around large boulders.

But will rocks be able to hide us from detection devices? Diego thought.

Unknown, Commander. We will find out.

They slowed as they approached the three lights. A movement above him caused Diego to look up where he saw Elder swimming by. Something flashed from near the lights and almost hit the Teeloss. At the last second, Elder jerked to the side and avoided the beam.

Diego heard a grinding groan, then a doorway or hatch opened. Several figures swam out in bulky suits carrying weapons. To his astonishment, Diego saw they were the same size and shape as him. They swam toward Elder and aimed their weapons. Diego opened his mouth to call out a warning, but

Elder disappeared. Blinking, Diego realized Elder didn't swim away. He just wasn't there anymore.

The three Amashina flitted around the two swimmers almost faster than Diego could make them out. Another flash from the swimmer's weapon, but Diego didn't think it connected with any of his Amashi friends. If he could just get in the building.

I think we can, Commander.

One of you must go back and tell Rreengrol what's going on. In case....

Fress will go back.

Diego could feel the young squire's disappointment.

Fress is a fast swimmer. She can get back to the spaceport quicker than anyone else. Go now!

She shot off, swallowed up in the darkness. Jeng swam toward the structure, close to the ocean floor. Bress followed, and then Diego.

They swam toward an opening. The two figures were still looking for any Amashina swimming nearby. Now, if they could get inside without being noticed.

Someone inside, Bress told him.

Let me go in first, then I'll signal you, Diego responded. He swam toward the opening and slipped in. He motioned to the Turengens, and they scooted through the hatch as well. Diego noticed buttons on the wall with symbols next to each one. He manually closed the hatch by pulling a handle. It closed with aggravating slowness, then stopped. He pulled again, and Bress and Jeng helped him. Jeng swam over to the buttons and studied them. Just as he reached to push one, the door closed faster, settling shut with a groan.

Diego watched the water cycle out of the chamber, and then he pulled the handle on the inner hatch. It slid open, and Jeng and Bress slipped into the inner room before it had completely opened. Diego heard a loud exclamation and then two thuds. He entered the inner chamber and saw two figures lying on the deck.

"How in the world did you do that?" he asked.

Bress pulled a small pistol out of his zippered pocket, giving Diego a toothy grin. "Knew it would work."

"Even with the underwater pressure?"

"Suit protects us. Why not protect the weapon?"

Diego nodded. "Duly noted, Commander." He kneeled to examine the two unconscious aliens and jerked back. They were identical—or almost identical. No wonder the Amashina had thought he might be an Old Enemy. These people were just like him. They were human!

He heard a noise behind him, the whooshing of water filling the outer hatch. "Their shipmates must be returning. We need to get out of sight."

"Need to move our prisoners first," Bress suggested.

"You're right. It wouldn't be wise for them to realize we're here." Diego opened each of the doors, but they were full of supplies. Then, they found a larger room containing seats, lights, and little else. A decompression chamber? He'd read about those. Regardless, it was the only place where they could hide. Diego dragged the two bodies in as the outer chamber emptied of water. The Turengens followed Diego and pulled the door behind them, almost shutting it. Diego heard soft noises from outside the door.

Confusion, wondering where these two went. Anger at the door shut in their faces.

Diego made no answer, mentally or aloud.

Taking off their suits and stowing them in the storage room. The door banged shut, then it grew quiet. *They are gone, as far as I can tell.*

Diego turned one alien over. It seemed strange calling these people alien when they looked so much like him. One had light hair, almost white, while the other one's longish hair had streaks of brown in it. Their skins were a shade lighter than his, but they had eyes, noses, mouths, and ears. Their noses were a little smaller than his, and their ears were lower on the sides of their heads. Hands and fingers were the same, except the digits were thinner. Two legs, smaller feet. Otherwise, he could have sworn he was looking at someone from his planet. Dress them in calzaneros, boots, cotton shirts, chaquetas, and a sombrero, and they would blend in with his people. Take the sombreros off and it would only be the hair making them stand out. Diego shook his head.

"Could they be from your planet? People you didn't know about?" Jeng asked in a soft voice.

CHAPTER FOURTEEN

"Anything is possible," Diego replied. "But no, I don't think there were any people on Earth who could fly out into space. I think these are the Old Enemy the Amashina mentioned."

"Probably, since they think you looked exactly like them. Personally, I see differences," Bress commented.

"We need to explore this ship, or whatever it is, before they catch us. I don't think we'll have much time. If discovered, split up, and try to get out and report to the Amashina."

"We are not big enough to work the hatch," Jeng pointed out.

"Use the levers if you can."

"Hard to reach, but we will do our best."

"We'll stay together as long as we can," Diego replied.

Bress nodded toward the captives. "What do we do with them?"

Diego looked around and saw nothing with which to tie them, so he jerked off their pants. He tied the stretchy material around their hands and pulled the ends up to tie gags. The Turengens did the same with the other prisoner. Diego opened the heavy door and peered out. Then he slipped into the room, listening.

"No one beyond the other door, Commander," Jeng said.

Diego opened the hatch and investigated the corridor. It extended in one direction, dimly lit. Perhaps these people needed little light to see. Diego motioned for the otter people to follow him. The helmet began collecting moisture inside, and he removed it. It stayed attached to his suit at the back of his neck. He wouldn't have to carry it.

Doors showed at precise intervals — regular doors. When they heard a noise ahead of them, Diego cracked a door and peered into the darkness. They slipped in and pulled the door shut behind them. Pulling out his small flashlight, Diego searched the room, stopping when he saw several bunks with mounds on them. He turned off the light and listened. The sleepers made soft sighs and snores. Bress gave him an all-clear signal, and they slipped back out into the corridor.

The trio continued, ducking into another room, when they heard sounds ahead of them. This was another storage room. Diego couldn't figure out what they were storing. Their lights showed boxes stacked and secured on one wall and equipment against another wall. The third wall had only a few medium-sized containers stacked on the deck. The fourth wall was bare, but dust patterns showed something had sat there not too long ago. A metal table was bolted to the floor on one side of the room.

Diego pulled a box toward him and examined it. He noticed symbols covering the sealed box, which had a handle at the top. "What is it?" he murmured.

"Could we unseal it?" Jeng asked.

Diego shook his head. They had to be sealed for a reason. Weapons? Before he could say a thing, he heard the door latch turning. Motioning behind the table, Diego turned off his light. The trio crouched as the door opened, and two crewmen entered. They turned on their dim lights and spoke to each other, but Diego couldn't understand any of it. Each gathered a box and left the room, the last one closing the door.

"Could you make out anything from their thoughts?" Diego asked. He had a very uneasy feeling about this.

"Commander, these are weapons! They are leaving them outside, where they explode. This will devastate the Amashina."

"What? Why would they do such a thing?"

"Because they are the 'old enemy'?"

"We can't let them do that!" Diego exclaimed.

"How do we stop them?" Bress asked.

Diego pondered. "If they can leave these devices outside on the ocean floor, then this ship must be able to vacate this area. Can a spaceship stay deep in the ocean?"

Jeng's whiskers wiggled as he thought. "I didn't think so, but maybe it can since this one appears to be a spaceship."

"So perhaps we need to find the control room and see if we can overpower the bridge crew. Can you figure out the controls if we did?"

Bress chittered. "We did with the Resh ship."

"Good. At the very least, we can put this ship out of commission."

Jeng listened with his telepathic sense and signaled when everything was clear. They crept through the shadowy hallways, up ladders, and into long corridors. The trio ducked into shadows when the ship's inhabitants came too close. Diego got the impression this ship didn't have a large complement. He hoped that would help them gain control. They couldn't let them blow up this world like the Amashina said they had done in the past.

"We must be getting near the control room," Diego whispered.

"Their thoughts are jumbled, making it hard to know for sure, but I believe we are. There are people working with the weapons and others who are in charge. Plus a few more who are sleeping. Close; we are close."

Diego only nodded and followed his Turengen comrades.

At the end of the corridor, they stopped in front of a locked door, showing a row of symbols in the alien language. Diego sucked in a deep breath. What to do now?

"We want to try something, Commander," Bress said.

"Go ahead."

Bress closed his eyes and concentrated. Diego kept his mind clear, hoping he wouldn't distract Bress.

It seemed a long time, but he heard a noise on the other side of the hatch-like door, and then the handle moved. The door creaked open. Diego flattened himself against the wall next to the door frame. Bress stood in front of the door as bold as a young rooster, chittering in the Seressin language. "You have stepped in something most foul."

Diego forced himself to keep a straight face as he stepped closer and grabbed the alien, jerking her out of the doorway. A girl? Bress fired his weapon, and the female slumped to the deck. His hand tingled from the shot, but Diego and the otter-men rushed in and saw four others sitting at various stations. Before the crewmembers could do more than shout at them, Bress had stunned them.

CHAPTER FIFTEEN

Pushing the door shut and pressing a button he hoped locked the door, Diego turned to the Turengen. They had pulled two of the crew out of their chairs and were studying the controls. The control room looked similar to what he was used to, except smaller.

Diego sat down in the captain's chair and pulled a screen closer to him. Symbols appeared and disappeared like flitting birds. He could make nothing of it. "Any luck?"

"Should have left one awake," Bress grumbled. "But think the blue button will do something."

Diego pushed the blue button. The ship shuddered until he released the button. Someone banged on the door. "Maybe there's your awake one." The Turengen dashed to the door and unlatched it. When he opened it, the woman they had stunned earlier stumbled in. Bress's weapon didn't have as much effect on these people. Still, Bress wanted someone whose mind he could read, and here she was.

Wrapping his arm around her waist, Diego pushed the door shut with his other arm and locked it. He didn't want to hurt her, but she was squirming and twisting like a madwoman.

She jerked away from him and stared first at the Turengen and then stared at him, her green eyes wide.

"I am sub-Commander Diego Perez. We are taking over your ship."

She spat out something Diego figured wasn't very nice. He wrapped his arms around her waist again, trying not to hurt her. She attempted kicking him in the knee, but he jerked to the side. Her foot stomped on his instep instead. He yelped and then snatched her leg. The young woman dropped to the ground, still kicking. Jeng dashed over and tried to grab her arm, but she was squirming so hard that all he got was some of her long, light-colored hair instead.

She screeched and gripped Jeng's leg, throwing him over her body and across the deck. Then Diego reached in, grabbed her arm, and pulled her to her feet. He wrapped his arms around her upper torso, pinning her arms to her side. Despite her kicking and fighting, he still didn't want to hurt her. "Can you...get any thoughts...from her? She's a wildcat!"

"Only that she wishes she had a weapon to blow your head off."

"Can you put something in her mind, Bress? A spaceship cruising in space or something to make her think of the controls for this one."

"Will try."

She kept struggling, then stopped for a moment before trying to escape again. "Stop!" Diego shouted in several languages. Jeng handed Bress's stun gun to Diego. "Stop!" He almost shoved the pistol in her face to make his point. She grabbed for it, and he fired a quick burst. She slumped to the deck but wasn't totally unconscious.

"Is there something we can use to restrain her? I can't keep this up."

Jeng tugged the girl's outer pants off and used them to tie her hands behind her back. Diego helped, feeling he was tying up an octopus. When they secured her, Diego picked her up and carried her to the control consoles. She tried to spit on him, but Diego ignored it; his hands were full. He dropped her on the seat. "I thought if she was sitting here, you might get something from her mind."

Someone banged on the door.

"Jeng, watch the door and shoot if they open it."

"Press the blue button again, Commander. Longer this time."

Diego did so, and the ship shuddered. Somewhere beneath their feet, engines roared. The vessel lifted from the ocean floor with a shudder. The girl struggled and almost fell out of her chair. Banging at the door continued as the ship rose. Soon, the small forward port changed from pitch dark to subdued light. A small computer screen near the controls showed how quickly they neared the surface. The pitch of the engines changed. The monitor showed the ship breaking free from the surface of the ocean and surging toward the sky. The banging had ceased.

Diego and Bress secured themselves in their chairs. Jeng fell to the floor and slid until he grabbed something. This ship had nothing to compensate for the excess gravity forces of a space-bound vessel. Diego tried to keep his finger on the button and keep conscious.

The girl remained conscious, gazing at him with a grim smile—or was it a grimace? The off-blue sky darkened, and the ship's engines eased their roaring thrust. Diego let go of the button, and the pounding in his head eased up to a pony galloping across his brain rather than a stallion. He sucked in his breath and felt muscles protesting. At least the ship had gravity now that they were in space. "Bress, Jeng, are you alright?"

"Yes, Commander, but prefer Seressin ships. Not so hard on the body."

The girl struggled with her bonds, almost falling out of her chair. Diego shook his head, and she stopped, staring at him.

Diego made a conglomeration of signs—a few he had learned back home on Earth, others with Phris when he was first captured, and times he'd been without a translator. She cocked her head and continued to gaze at him, a slight smile playing about her lips. He repeated his signs, asking if they had a translator so they could understand each other.

Finally, she said something sounding like the cross between a cricket and a hissing cat and motioned her head toward a console. Diego slid out of his chair and shuffled over to the one he thought she had referred to, pointing. The girl made a different noise and then shrugged. Frustrated, Diego began pantomiming again.

"Translator is on that console," Bress said. "But a shrug is 'yes' in her culture. Nodding is 'no.'"

"Oh." Diego pointed to each switch and waited. She nodded until, finally, she shrugged. "Bress?"

"Hard to tell, but I don't feel deception."

Diego pushed the button. A light blinked at the edge of the console near the switch. He looked and found something resembling a learning helmet hanging on a hook. When he glanced at the girl, she was shrugging.

Diego studied the helmet. He pantomimed, putting it on. She shrugged again. Bress didn't warn him, so Diego slipped it on.

The girl spoke as soon as he had it over his ears. After a brief pause, he heard words he understood. "Who are you? Who are those with you? My people will make you a prisoner. Why did you come and take over our ship? Where do you come from?"

Diego held up his hands to fend off her questions. Then he nodded. She stopped. "Bress, check our other friends and make sure they don't surprise us while I am talking to this one."

Her eyes widened, and she opened her mouth to speak again. Diego nodded his head. She waited. "My name is Diego Perez, Sub-Commander in the Seressin Empire under High Commander Ziron. These are part of my crew. They are Turengens."

"You use inferior creatures as crew?" she asked.

"Inferior? Hardly." But he wouldn't elaborate, not wishing to give away some of their attributes. "Who are you, and why did your people invade the Amashi oceans?"

"Invade?" She snorted. "We are here to get what we left behind many years ago."

"If your people left something so long ago, why didn't you ask the Amashina. They could have helped you find it."

"You are talking about the fish?"

"I am talking about the intelligent ocean people," Diego replied, realizing he spoke to a more xenophobic people, much like he had been before he made friends with so many intelligent beings.

"How can you call a fish intelligent?"

Diego countered. "Who do you think built the spaceport? The Amashina designed it. They worked with other races to build something many inhabitants of the galaxy could visit." He paused. "The Amashina leadership gave me this suit that provides me so much freedom in the ocean...."

"We do not need help," she snapped.

"But your means of getting what you want is destroying some of the Amashina's living spaces. And by now...."

The banging started on the door again. Jeng pattered over to watch for anyone entering. Two more of the spaceship's inhabitants were waking. Bress only glanced at them to make sure they were still secure, and then he returned his concentration to the consoles and computers.

"They will get in. I told you my people would capture you and make you prisoner," she said with a cocky grin.

CHAPTER SIXTEEN

"They will not get in right away." At least, Diego hoped they wouldn't. "We have time to talk."

Her frown had disappeared. She studied him as though trying to figure Diego out. "Are you one of the outlanders?"

Diego shook his head. "No, I'm not. What is it you want to recover?"

"The remains of our people attacked by the creatures of this planet."

"The Amashina do not know what destroyed the people of long ago. They remember a massive sun-like fireball that blew away most of the land area."

"A fireball?" she asked in a whisper. The frown reappeared. "That's what they told you?"

"Yes. The Amashina are intelligent and have retold the story for so long they were wondering if it was just their imagination. Or if there ever had been a landrace living on Amashi. It startled them when I arrived with my crew for an official visit." Diego took a breath. "Are your people called Trologs?"

She stared at him, her eyes widening. The computer translator didn't change the name, so Diego figured he was right.

"Yes. You say who you are, but what are you? Except for minor differences, you look exactly like us."

"I'm a human. In one of Earth's languages, it is Homo sapiens. I am the only member of my race in the Seressin Empire."

She cocked her head to the side again. "Why is that? Did your people die?"

He smiled. "No, a Seressin ship visited my planet and captured me. They were curious about humans. I have worked since my capture and become a sub-commander in the Seressin Defense forces."

"These Seressin sound powerful. What are they like?"

"They are reptilians. They are strong, have thick skins, and short tempers."

"Why would they want you as one of their war leaders?"

Diego laughed. "They think I'm clever, brave, and lucky."

She gave him a slight smile. Then asked, "Are you?"

"I imagine so. I am still here."

The banging on the door increased in volume and intensity. The other Trologs inside the control room were struggling against their bonds.

"Commander! Jeng! Grab onto something." Bress called out.

Diego snapped the restraints around the girl and then dropped into the nearest chair, jerking the straps around his torso. Jeng scurried for the nearest seat. Before he could buckle the straps tight, the engines roared back to life, and the ship dropped into the upper atmosphere. They rolled into a fast spin, and Diego wondered if Bress was trying to break his neck. The Trolog woman screamed once and then clamped her lips together. The engines squealed in agony.

"Are you going to slow down?" Diego got out. "Or are we going to splatter all over the surface of the ocean?"

"Patience, Commander."

The ship flashed through the middle atmosphere into the lower atmosphere. The bow thrusters fired, and Diego felt the ship slow. Bress fired other jets, and the ship turned back toward space.

"I think I got through to Fress, telling her to send Rreengrol up in our cruiser to pick us up. I didn't want this ship back on Amashi with the explosives on board, but I needed to disorient them so I could contact Fress." Bress ducked his head. "Sorry, I didn't warn you, Commander."

"No problem, Bress. You acted. But it's too bad we can't dump those explosives."

"We could, but we would have to fight the crew to do it," Bress pointed out. "There's no way to do it from here."

Diego thought of something from his training. "Bress, is it possible for Rreengrol and Fress to pilot our cruiser alone?"

Bress chittered something in the Turengen language and then sighed. "No."

Diego glanced over at the young woman. She was unconscious. He hadn't even found out her name. Then he realized his duty entailed finding out more about her people, their agenda, and where they came from. She told him a little, but he needed to know more.

"Is there a way to jettison those explosives out here without dealing with the crew? That would allow us to land at the spaceport."

Bress sighed. "Perhaps."

"I need to try talking to our friends." Unbuckling his safety straps, Diego made his way over to the girl. She was waking up.

"Going into the upper atmosphere, Commander."

"Thanks, Bress. Continue."

The girl opened her eyes and stared at him. Diego saw how intensely green and beautiful they were. He pulled himself back to matters at hand. "We are going back into space where the weapons your people brought can't harm the planet below. I would like to know a little more about you and your people. Maybe I can talk to your leaders in the future."

Her expression grew hard again. "Why? So, all these underwater creatures can conquer us? Or your Seressin can overrun our planet and cities?"

"No, but your people have landed on a Seressin-held planet. Then you started destroying some of the planet's habitats and killing her people. Perhaps we could negotiate and come to an agreement that would save lives." Diego knew he was pushing the limits of his authority — he probably had exceeded them — but Marix Ziron wasn't here, and these Trologs were. "Seressin are warlike and have some ferocious enemies, but they are loyal to their friends and allies. Perhaps your leaders might consider an alliance?"

She snorted and then stopped. "What would you offer?"

Diego laughed. "I am a sub-commander. I can offer nothing except the goodwill of my commanders. However, with their goodwill also comes the benefits of commerce and the protection of a powerful group of people."

"People? We are people! These others are creatures."

"You didn't include me in that."

"That's because you aren't a creature. You look just like us."

"That's the point. I am not just like you. I came from a different planet — a very primitive planet."

She shook her head. "No, your hair and eyes are different." She pointed to Bress and Jeng. "They are animals."

Diego sighed. "I had that attitude a year and a half ago. I have learned a lot since then. Are you willing to learn?"

"I...." She stopped and gazed at him and then at the Turengen. "Is it piloting our ship?"

Diego nodded. At her frown, he remembered the Trolog 'yes' sign and shrugged. "Yes, he is. Despite not knowing your written language, he is intelligent enough to figure out machines, including spaceships. All his people are smart that way."

She continued studying the Turengen but then nodded. "That is hard to believe. I am willing to learn, but that might mean nothing since I am not in charge either."

"Will they treat my two crewmembers like diplomats with dignity and respect?"

"I can't make that kind of promise. I am only the captain's daughter."

Diego raised his eyebrows in surprise. "Which one is your father?" he asked, pointing to the Trologs lying bound on the deck.

The girl didn't hesitate. "He is," she answered, pointing to the one nearest Diego.

He glanced at Bress, who made a slight shake of his head. "No, he isn't." What kind of game was she playing?

CHAPTER SEVENTEEN

Treela's eyes varied between Diego and the Turengen. He was sure she had seen Bress's signal.

Then Jeng approached a different Trolog and untied him. "This one is the captain," he said.

The girl gaped. "How…."

"I told you they were smart."

The captain rose to his feet, his eyes never leaving Diego's. "Why did you take over my ship? You had no right."

"As a commander of the Seressin Empire Defense Force, I had all the rights in the world, sir. This planet is a member planet of the empire, and your explosives were causing damage to the planet and its inhabitants."

The captain sneered. "You talk like they are intelligent? They are animals."

"Please, I already discussed that with your daughter. I will be happy to turn your ship back over to you, one commander to another, if you treat us as emissaries. I am only interested in discussion, not fighting."

The captain nodded, a frown still plastered across his face. "Those so-called inhabitants destroyed an entire colony of our ancestors."

Diego also nodded, letting the captain know he didn't agree with him. "Their history doesn't agree, but that's something we can discuss later."

"So, you give my ship back to me, and we're supposed to treat you like some kind of royalty instead of the pirates you are."

"No, not royalty, but as intelligent people from one empire to intelligent people of another empire. I realize you can do whatever you want, but I am curious, and I hope you are curious enough to want to learn more about those I work with."

The captain nodded again. "No, I don't. We came to get anything remaining of the Trolog settlement we could find and then...."

"Then seek retribution?" Diego said. "I can't imagine the explosives you carry in your hold were there to open graves. They are too powerful. It would blow any Trolog remains surviving through the years into powder."

The Trolog captain glared at him for a moment.

The captain's daughter shrugged. "That's all the teachers tell us."

"Treela, that is enough!"

So now Diego had her name. "The Amashina did nothing to your ancestors. They were as puzzled by the explosions as you were. That destruction not only killed all your colonists but wiped out the only large land mass on this planet. Why didn't you contact the leadership here and ask for their help?"

"From fish?"

Diego sighed. "Yes, fish. They are also intelligent life forms. There are many species of intelligent ocean lifeforms on Amashi, and they all get along. Wouldn't you like to know such diverse species?"

"Yes!" Treela replied, her shoulders jerking up and down in vigorous shrugs.

"You are here to observe, not decide, daughter! Apparently, your empire allows children to make important decisions," the captain snapped.

Diego felt the warmth rise on his cheeks. "I gained my status as commander of this mission based on my success on other missions."

Treela struggled against her bonds. "I am curious about this empire that has so many diverse members. Do you have women in your military?"

Diego was glad he didn't mention his time as a slave. "Yes. That is a new improvement."

Commander, Rreengrol has matched orbit with this ship. He and Fress were able to bring our cruiser into space. Not sure how, Bress told him.

Shut this ship down. That should give us time to make it out of here and back to our vessel.

Bress shut down most of the ship's systems, leaving only life-support, and grabbed hold of the console when they lost artificial gravity. The captain stumbled, and his feet floated out from under him. The other crewmembers wiggled and jerked, trying to loosen their bonds.

Diego grabbed Treela's chair to limit movement. His team members' skills continued amazing him. "Captain, I suggest you check your monitor. You'll notice a very well-armed and fast starship off your port bow."

The captain 'swam' to the console, trying very hard to ignore Bress. He typed up something on his computer and the main monitor showed Diego's ship.

Diego continued. "That's what some commanders call a pocket battlecruiser. It does short missions to various worlds within the Seressin Empire. Even though we don't expect trouble, we are ready if it comes to us." *Bress, tell me what Treela's thinking. Is it safe to untie her?*

She is curious about you. Very curious. The best I am picking up is that she doesn't think you'd hurt her. She is also tired of her father telling her what to do. She finds opportunity in our presence.

Diego unbuckled Treela and untied her bonds.

The captain stared at him.

"And before you talk about lesser creatures, Bress, here, and Jeng are my navigators. Good ones, too. Even the Seressin didn't realize how good they were until recently. We are returning to our ship."

Diego stood as straight as zero gravity afforded him. "Captain, as commander of this mission, I request permission to accompany you back to your home world as an emissary of the Seressin High Command."

The Trolog captain didn't answer unless a glower was the answer.

Bress unbuckled and slid out of the seat, pushing himself toward the doorway. Jeng followed. The captain slid into the seat Bress had abandoned. The other crewmembers struggled against their bonds.

Treela maneuvered toward him. Diego hoped he wouldn't have to fight his way out of the control room. It would be hard enough getting from one ship to the other. The girl grabbed onto his arm. "I'm going with you."

"What?" her father cried. He nodded several times.

"If they are coming to Trologar, they need someone on board to ensure their safe arrival," Treela said.

She also likes you, Commander. And finds you fascinating.

Diego had not thought of what Treela or Bress were saying. He felt his cheeks warming again and didn't respond to Bress. "Treela, we will treat you well." Bress opened the door, and Diego used his stun weapon on the two Trologs trying to get in. They sagged against the bulkhead and then floated upward.

Treela pulled on him, and they swam down the corridor to an elevator. She would have to get a space suit, so he let her lead the way, hoping his trust in her wouldn't backfire.

CHAPTER EIGHTEEN

Diego felt a slight shift in his belly just before gravity returned. He had enough forewarning to get his feet under his body. It still jarred his knee joints. Bress and Jeng touched the floor as though they did this every day. Treela motioned them to follow her. She dashed into the elevator. Punching a few buttons, the door slid shut, and the elevator moved sideways. When it stopped, Treela stepped out first. Only one crewmember faced them, and Diego subdued him with his stun gun.

Diego recognized the area where they had entered the ship. "Bress, can you still reach Fress?"

"Yes. She says the ship is powering up. Rreengrol asks permission to fire a warning shot."

"He has it."

Treela pulled a spacesuit from a rack and motioned for them to find suits for themselves.

The ship shuddered. "Bress," Diego began, pointing to the skin-tight deep-sea outfit he wore. "Do you think these would be suitable for space since they work deep underwater?"

"Maybe. Except the problem would be air. In the ocean, the suits pull air from the water. There will be nothing to pull air from unless the suit can store it before going out."

"We will not test that idea. Grab a couple of smaller Trolog spacesuits and put them on over your Amashina outfit."

Diego pulled off the translating device and attached the Amashina helmet. He immediately received the ship's chatter from his ship. "Rreengrol?"

"Diego!"

"We are coming over as soon as we get the spacesuits on."

"The ship has powered down again. I think they believed us," Rreengrol said with a laugh. "Hurry, I need more hands here. My tail hurts."

Rreengrol's comment puzzled Diego, but he figured it out and grinned. Then he wondered about Trolog armaments. He turned to Treela. "The explosives!" Diego realized he wasn't using the translator, but she must have understood him.

She made motions for him to follow her. He hesitated only a moment. Treela had come to their side quickly, and Diego wondered if he was too quick to trust her despite what Bress had told her before.

Bress helped him out on this one. *No, commander. She hates the explosives.*

Not far down the corridor was the weapons room. They were already on rolling carts. "We're going to jettison these explosives as we leave, Rreengrol. Make sure the Trologs don't fire on us." They dashed back to the room with the extra suits.

"We'll watch for any weaponry signals and fire another shot to warn them if they do."

"Good." Diego grabbed a bigger suit and slid into it. He wasn't sure where his fins were, but he couldn't worry about that. Diego had to remove his Amashina helmet; it wouldn't fit inside the Trolog space helmet. Hopefully, he'd be able to hang on to it in transit. Diego helped the Turengens with their oversized suits. Treela made sure he was ready.

The young commander signed to Treela, asking if she was all set. She shrugged. They ran as fast as they could to the room with the weapons. Then, they each wheeled a cart to the hatch. He cycled the door open, and they entered. It was a tight fit with the carts, but they made it.

Diego set the mechanism to siphon out all the air. The double suits held up well. Treela pushed the buttons to open the outer hatch. Diego and the others pushed the carts out of the airlock, where they floated in silent majesty away from the ship.

Treela pointed to the controls on the front of her suit and pushed some of them. Small puffs of air propelled her toward the Seressin ship. Diego pointed to similar buttons on his suit. Treela nodded. Diego reached to push the button, but Treela grabbed his hand. She pointed to a different button and then gave an exaggerated shrug. Diego shrugged, too, and pushed the right button.

Diego peeled off his Trolog suit as soon as air had siphoned into the outer hatch. He pressed the controls to open the inner hatch. "Fress, can you open communications with Commander Ziron?"

"Will be ready for you, Commander."

Diego left the Trolog helmet inside the hatch, then he sprinted the short distance to the control room. The others pattered behind him. The door slid open, and Rreengrol greeted him from the navigator's chair. He slid out for Bress to take over and took the weaponry console.

"I have an open link to *Star Devourer*, Commander."

"Thanks, Fress. And get a translator for our visitor."

Treela studied every aspect of the room, her green eyes wide. She stared at Rreengrol. Diego motioned for her to come closer. He tapped his access code into the computer.

In a moment, Ziron gazed at him from the monitor. "Diego, I have heard disturbing things going on out there."

Diego gave Marix Ziron the condensed version of what happened on Amashi. "May I have permission to accompany the Trolog ship to its home world and see if these people wish to ally themselves with the Seressin Empire? That way, I can find out their history with the Amashi world, too."

"What is to stop them from taking you and the others prisoner?"

"The daughter of the ship's captain is with us."

Ziron scratched his cheek patch. "And is this daughter of value to them?"

"That is my understanding, Marix."

The reptilian scratched the other cheek patch, considering Diego's request. "Activate the sensors and proceed with all due caution."

"Yes, Marix. It will be done."

Treela had approached Diego's console, much like a mouse trying to grab corn from under a sleeping cat. He kept his eyes on the monitor and his commanding officer but also noted the Trolog girl. "Come and meet my commander, Marix Ziron, captain of the ship *Star Devourer*."

She stepped forward, and her jaw dropped.

"Commander Ziron, this is Treela of Trologar."

"Obviously not familiar with the Seressin Empire," Ziron commented with a bark of laughter.

"No, sir."

"I greet you, Lady Treela. My sub-commander will take good care of you."

"Th...thank you, Commander Ziron."

"Carry on, Diego."

"Yes, sir." The connection ended.

"He is your commander?"

"Yes. All of us on this ship are under his command. We are soldiers, warriors in the Seressin Empire."

"How big is this empire?" she asked.

"I've never counted or asked, but there are more than a hundred star systems I know of."

"And your home world is part of that empire?"

"No. I was, uh, recruited there. I am the only human in the empire."

"Yes, that's right. You said that." She paused a moment and then added, "I wasn't just curious. I thought you'd have a better chance of not being attacked since I am here."

"I know, Treela. What is your father's name? I would like to address him properly."

"Captain Trillin Tremorin."

"There is a message from the Trolog ship, Commander," Fress announced.

Language translation was built into the communicator and was almost instantaneous. "This is Commander Perez. What can I do for you, Captain Tremorin?"

"I am ordering my daughter to be returned to our ship," he replied.

Treela stood next to him. "I am returning home on Commander Perez's ship. I am being well treated."

"You are my daughter. You need to obey. This is an order from the planetary leadership."

"I would like to see other inhabitants of our galaxy and decide on my own whether to like them. I don't need a teacher telling me to look down on every creature except our kind."

Diego figured he'd better try to diffuse this argument. "Captain, you have my word that your daughter will be safe. As long as no one tries to destroy us." He waited a few beats for that to sink in. "She will also teach us the protocol and customs of your people so that we can greet them properly and not cause offense."

"It is a little late for that," Tremorin growled. "And I will not deal with an alien pup who should still be in school rather than pretending to command a spaceship, no matter that he looks like us."

He felt a flush of anger, but Diego did not respond. The communications screen shut off.

CHAPTER NINETEEN

Diego looked up at Treela. "He wouldn't fire on us, would he?" He raised his eyes to Rreengrol in an unspoken order.

Tears brimmed in her eyes. "I didn't think so." She blinked them away. "I guess he will not give you the coordinates for our home world. And I guess...."

"Commander," Bress interrupted. "The other ship has engaged its sub-light engines and is pulling away."

"Stay a safe distance aft with shields up. Make sure you're recording coordinates."

"Yes, sir."

"They're leaving me," came her soft voice through the translator. "I shouldn't have come."

"We'll make sure you get home, if not right now, then later," he assured her, wondering if he was making a rash promise.

"What father would leave his daughter in an unknown place?" she cried.

"One obeying commands from his superiors. I should have realized that. I focused on meeting new people—people who look like me." He *was* a pup, in this case, letting his emotions get in the way.

"They found a gate. They're gone," Fress announced.

"Is it a recorded gate?"

"No, Commander. Should we go through?" Bress asked.

"Yes."

He felt the slide and pull of going through a gate. When they had made the transfer, they found themselves in what Diego could only describe as a dead area, with only the wormhole gate behind them and distant stars ahead. Very distant. There was no other ship. "How many gates did you come through to get to Amashi?"

She tapped her chin and said, "We went through at least two. It was a course that an ancient astronomer had figured out." She sniffed and then sighed.

"Slow," Diego ordered, realizing that anything further might get them lost. "I think we need to go back and study the information we have — see what you remember."

"Yes," she agreed. "I wish I had paid better attention in class."

"We have a robot teacher who might help if we go back to Marix Ziron's ship."

"I was told there was a huge cache of information on... Amashi, you call it, that the ancients left before they were destroyed. I don't know if it's true or not."

"Seriously? So, you meant to use the explosives to expose old artifacts?"

She shrugged, even as a tear slid down her cheek. "The instruments detected nothing, so then the secondary mission kicked in. To destroy the creatures that wiped out our people."

"Oh." He sat in his command chair and studied the monitor. All the information Bress and Fress had gathered flashed across his screen. Regardless of what they could do on Amashi or on the ship, they couldn't stay where they were. "Return to Amashi after you have gathered all possible information."

"Yes, Commander."

Diego rubbed the back of his neck. "I will report to Marix Ziron when we land." He didn't think the commander would be thrilled.

CHAPTER TWENTY

Diego was right. Marix Ziron wasn't happy. When he gave a full report from the privacy of his cabin after they landed back on Amashi, Ziron paused for several moments. He first rubbed one cheek patch and then the other.

"Quirlis," he began, glaring into the monitor of the portable computer. "Do you believe this Captain Tremorin will return for his daughter?"

The harsh tone stung Diego. "I don't know, Commander, but I believe, since they were ready for revenge against the Amashina, that he will return."

"With an invasion force?"

Diego took a deep breath. "That possibility crossed my mind, Marix."

"If you are a smart commander, it should have," Ziron growled. "Their desire for revenge implies an upcoming attack. What action do you think needs to be taken in response to it?"

"Treela said there was some kind of cache of scientific knowledge that her people had left on this planet. Perhaps it would have the information on how to find her planet."

"And invade before they do?"

Diego composed himself for a few seconds before answering. "No, sir. To return Treela to her people to show our goodwill." Ziron blinked in surprise. "With a couple of ships to enforce that goodwill, if need be, as we return the Trolog citizen."

"Hmmph. I think we should teach them a lesson for the damage they did on a Seressin planet, but we can leave that for now. Can you figure out where this system is if you don't find the information you are looking for?"

"I have sent all the data we gathered when we tried the gate the Trolog ship went through. I hope the technicians back on the *Devourer* can work on it. Also, there was an ion trail, but it was tenuous."

"Go back and check it out. Get the Amashi to search for this cache. It might have more value than just the location of a small empire."

"Yes, sir."

"And Diego...." Ziron paused and cleared his throat, which was a little out of character for him.

"Yes, Marix?"

"Do not get caught up in the fact these people look like you. Do not let that interfere with your mission. Never let that interfere with your duty and loyalty!"

Commander Ziron could have been reading his mind. "I understand, and I will obey. I am an officer in the Seressin Empire."

Ziron nodded. "Well answered, Diego. I must admit, by humanoid standards, she seems an intelligent girl. Don't let her distract you. I don't need to remind you of all you have accomplished in two solar cycles."

"Thank you, Marix."

"I will send a ship out there. There needs to be someone waiting if these people decide to return. I may even come out myself, depending on the disposition of the Serix."

"Yes, sir."

"Carry on."

"Yes, Commander." The connection ended. Diego remembered what he had accomplished, and he was proud of it. He also realized what he had missed, but he could do nothing about it.

Diego left his cabin and found the Turengen and Treela lounging in the common area. He could see the fatigue etched in their faces, so he knew going back out now would be counterproductive. A visit with the Amashi leadership was in order. "Tomorrow, at first light, we're going out to explore where Treela's father disappeared. That will give us time to rest and have a good meal. I'm going to see the Amashi and convey a message from Commander Ziron. Get a head start on that rest."

Thankfully, the meeting didn't take long. The Amashi agreed with Commander Ziron to send out explorers to study the vicinity of the earthquakes with more advanced detection devices. Diego headed back to their suite of rooms, satisfied.

Rrishan, released from the medical bay, paced the floor of the common room when Diego returned. Rreengrol sat on the overlarge lounging chair, watching her. "Welcome back. You look about as tired as I feel."

One of the cabin doors slid open, and Treela walked out, rubbing her eyes. She stared at the Grrlock squire. Rrishan did the same with Treela.

"Do these people come from your world, Commander?" Treela asked, keeping formal.

"No," he answered, introducing Treela to Rrishan.

Treela still wore the portable translator so she could follow the conversation. "You are of the same species as Rreengrol?"

Rrishan nodded. "I am of the same family. I'm his little sister."

That began a friendship Diego welcomed. He didn't know how long it would be before he could get Treela home—if at all. Fress, Jeng, and Bress joined them, and the seven chatted until mealtime.

The dinner was delicious, but Diego felt exhaustion creep into his mind and body. His recent decisions also weighed him down. They returned to the suite. While Diego craved sleep, at first, it didn't come. Finally, though, he fell asleep, and as he often did when stressed, he dreamed.

CHAPTER TWENTY-ONE

Underwater. They were below the depth where they had found the Trolog ship. Many of the creatures had spots and lines along their bodies that lit up. Eyes, tails, fins, stripes along their sides, strange dangling things where the ends lit like miniature lanterns. Long sea snakes slid across the bottom and rose to check them out, grimacing with vast mouths full of teeth. Diego saw variants of the tentacled people shooting through the water with some kind of propulsion, enormous eyes gazing at him.

Rreengrol and the Turengens were with him, along with the Amashina leadership. Diego noticed someone else, and he recognized Treela, swimming along as though she had grown up in a water environment. They followed the sea floor as it sloped even deeper. The Amashina stationed themselves ahead, behind, and to the side. They must have excellent eyesight because they didn't use any lights like he and his companions did. Diego heard strange sounds that he realized were noises from their escorts. It puzzled him.

Everything seemed fine — the sea calm. Then, a creature exploded up from below. It snatched one of the Amashina. Something smashed into his side. Diego dropped his light, and all he could hear was the roar of something huge. A tentacle wrapped around his middle, jerking him farther down in the dark. He heard other strange sounds, but they sounded frantic.

Diego could still breathe, but the pressure around his diaphragm intensified. He tried to push the tentacle away, but it was like pushing a shuttle across the sand. It continued to draw him downward. His ears popped, but they kept going farther and farther. He heard Jeng and Fress calling in his mind. Then the creature jerked him into a hole and through a cave that had some of the dim light creatures on its walls.

The "cave" turned out to be a rough, cylindrical structure, leading him to the realization that this was not a cave at all! Something someone built. Someone had built it!

Diego jerked awake, panting. Was this another warning like on Koress? Was this something that knowing made it possible to change? The cylinder could be from the Trologs—the 'Old Enemy.' This time, they would be more prepared. Diego padded to the bathroom and took care of his business, then tried to sleep again. He stared at the ceiling for a long time.

CHAPTER TWENTY-TWO

"Are you planning on waking up in time for breakfast, or do you like those wonderful sustenance bars so much you're going to wait until we're on the ship?" Rreengrol stood in the doorway, already dressed.

"Had trouble getting to sleep."

"Seems to be common with commanders. Come on; it'll be okay. It isn't the first time Marix Ziron gnawed on you. And it won't be the last. We'll get the readings and then come back and search for that lost Trolog base or artifacts or whatever it is. I'm even looking forward to a swim — even with my tail cramped up in the Amashi suit."

Diego smiled. "They didn't want some predator eating it. I am told that being tail-less in Grrlock society is degrading."

Rreengrol grimaced. "Hurry, they won't keep breakfast warm forever."

"You just like the idea of having fish for breakfast." Still, Diego cleaned up and dressed in record time — the food here was superb.

Treela stayed behind with Rrishan, who promised to teach her some of the Seressin language.

The rest manned the small spaceship and headed out to the gate. The computer made slight adjustments in their navigation, and they shot through with only a slight feeling of disorientation. "Take us to where we left off pursuit," Diego ordered. "Then we'll let the computers search for any clues."

"Based on trajectories, we are following the likely path," Bress reported a short time later.

"Keep it slow." Something bothered Diego. The hairs on

the back of his neck rose.

They crawled ahead, the computer picking up very little, but just enough to entice them further out into what Diego was seeing as a between space. When he examined the phenomena, the computer explained they were traversing an area between star systems. It wasn't empty, but it seemed that way.

Then, the monitor flashed something ahead. "All stop," he called out. The forward thrusters gave a quick burst to slow them further, then another to come as close to a stop as possible. The flash appeared on the monitor, still coming closer to them. Bress chittered a Turengen curse.

Diego understood what Bress said. "Reverse full!" The forward engines flared, but not enough. The ship shook like they had run into a wall. Then the lights went out. Emergency lights, along with the beeping from several consoles, told him the ship had met with a major obstacle. *But what?* "Is everyone all right?"

Three Turengen voices and Rreengrol's growl told him the crew was uninjured. Diego hoped the same held true of the ship. "Hull integrity?"

"No breach," Rreengrol said.

Diego breathed a sigh of relief. "Do we have any power at all?"

"We have auxiliary power," Bress reported. "Enough for life support and some thrust."

"Take us back to the other gate. We can get into spacesuits if need be. Bress, can you get our engines back online?"

"I will try, Commander."

"Fress and Jeng, help him. Rreengrol, keep an eye out for whoever set that surprise. What was it, anyway?"

"A force shield. This one was non-detectable until we were right on top of it," Bress explained.

Rreengrol growled deep in his throat. "I suspect the Trolog captain left it behind in case we tried to follow."

Diego felt disgusted that, again, he had made the wrong choice. "You're probably right, but watch for any other traps. Do our shields work? Or weapons?"

Again, Bress reported the dismal facts. "Shields are inoperative until we get our power core back online. Same with weapons. We can work on the engines to get us back to Amashi."

"I agree," Diego replied.

"At least we have an idea where Treela's father went," Rreengrol said.

Diego did, too, but he didn't want a Trolog battle cruiser coming through the other gate to prove the fact. He also worried the force shield might send a message to the Trologs, revealing Diego had triggered it. He felt like a rabbit in a trap, waiting for someone to come and snatch him up for dinner.

CHAPTER TWENTY-THREE

After several nerve-wracking hours, during which Diego checked and rechecked settings on the computer, Bress came out from under the console, chittering his success. "Not much, but we have minimum power to go along with the auxiliary power."

Diego pushed away from the weaponry console where he had been helping Rreengrol. "Take us through the gate and back to Amashi. Do we have the power to come in safely to the landing field?"

"Yes, Commander."

Diego studied the read-outs. "Fress, as soon as we pass through the gate, send a message to the Amashi spaceport. We are returning in a damaged craft. Request landing near a maintenance facility."

"Yes, sir."

In the time to reach Amashi, Diego typed up a report and sent it to Commander Ziron. The Marix wouldn't be happy about this, either, but his commander didn't respond other than to say he was glad there were no casualties.

They landed late into the night. Diego sealed the ship, and they trudged back to their temporary quarters. Rrishan and Treela were already in their cabins asleep. Despite what had happened, Diego didn't take long to fall asleep. No dreams bothered him.

When he got up the next morning, breakfast was waiting for him in the common area. Rreengrol also looked as though he had just awakened. Rrishan and Treela watched them. "As soon as we finish, we'll give you a status report," Diego said.

"I am glad you came back uninjured." Then Treela gave him a greeting in Seressin.

"You've been taking lessons!"

"From Rrishan. She's an excellent teacher."

Diego debriefed them on what happened on the other side of the gate.

"I didn't know, Commander," Treela said, her expression showing her consternation.

"What were you doing on your father's ship?" Diego asked. "You didn't seem to be a crewmember."

"I was a weelix. From what you've told me, it's like a position below one of your squires. It's a common practice for a coming-of-age Trolog to go with each parent to their duty stations and decide which one they prefer. I was on the ship to see if I wanted to be a captain. My mother is a teacher, and I had already been with her. I certainly didn't want to teach stuff I didn't think was true."

Diego's curiosity continued to prod him. "What if you didn't care for either parent's job?"

"I would submit a form to the commissioner of jobs, requesting a waiver, stating what I would prefer."

"Oh."

"But it's discouraged. A child is supposed to follow a father or mother. At least these days, a girl may follow her father. In the past, they discouraged even that."

"Did you want to follow your father?"

"Yes. I enjoyed seeing the stars." She paused and ducked her head. "But I think I have destroyed any chance for either job. They will reeducate me when I get home, and the government will select my lifework."

Diego felt sympathy for her. He had little future in California. Most likely, he would end up being a vaquero or a soldier somewhere even more primitive than where he'd grown up. Maybe get some land if he was lucky enough to keep everything he earned. "You could always become a squire here."

"Rrishan hinted such a thing, but I am not sure I am ready to abandon my home world."

"I understand. At least you can help us search for your people's artifacts until we figure out how to get you back."

She looked up at all of them and shrugged. She followed with a 'thank you' in Seressin.

When he went into his cabin to change into a clean set of clothes, a request from Commander Ziron waited for him. Diego didn't look forward to it, but, to his surprise, when he opened the link to Marix Ziron, the Seressin wasn't angry. He looked rather happy, in fact.

"Commander, I read your report, which was very thorough, by the way."

"Thank you, Marix."

"It would seem the Trologs have come close to a declaration of war."

"Close, Marix, but am I permitted to explain why I don't think we should take a fleet into the Trolog system?"

"Proceed, Diego."

"They may be afraid of us already, which is why they placed a defensive barrier at the second gate."

"Continue."

"If we can find what they were looking for here, then we have something to negotiate besides having one of their own people. It might be better to form an alliance with them or see if they want to join the Seressin Empire rather than going in and conquering them. If they were traveling in space for this length of time, perhaps they have something of use to the empire." Diego paused, and Ziron motioned him to continue. "Still, I wouldn't doubt they are gathering their warships to battle us. It might be a better advantage for us to wait for them."

"Then there should be a force of ships to greet them," Ziron growled.

"Yes, sir, but as a deterrent."

Ziron rubbed his cheek patch. "Very well. Proceed with the exploration. It will take a little time to gather warships. In the meantime, you will explore, and I will decide if we wait for the Trologs to bring their war to us or if we take it to them. If you find anything of value in the ocean, the Seressin Empire gets fifty percent. You and your team get ten percent, and the Trologs will reap thirty percent, depending on their behavior."

"What about the other ten percent, Marix?"

"For the Amashi government. Maybe they can enlarge that spaceport of theirs." Ziron barked a laugh.

Diego smiled. "Thank you, Marix."

"Happy hunting, Diego."

"Yes, sir."

CHAPTER TWENTY-FOUR

Feelona and Flash greeted Diego and his team. Bress stayed behind with the ship repair crew to supervise. The team was down to four.

"We found nothing near the Trolog ship's hiding place," Feelona said. "However, I re-examined the memories passed down to me when I became a leader. I was looking for any clues overlooked through the generations. We believe we know the location of the alien land dwellers' destroyed city. The one that exploded with sun-like power. It may be deeper and farther out to sea than you and your companions can swim."

"How much deeper can we go?" Diego asked.

"We do not know your range. The suits should be adaptable to any depth, but you will need to be aware of how your bodies feel as we go deeper."

"And how do we compensate for the distance?"

"That is what the surface craft is for," she said, pointing with one flipper toward a vessel bobbing at the dock. It looked much like boats Diego had seen before his abduction, except this one didn't have a sail. A triangular-shaped robot waited near the bow.

"If you're ready, I am." Diego swam over to the boat and hauled himself up a short ladder. He swung over the rail to a seat just inside and placed his underwater laser rifle under the seat. He had ordered weapons as a precaution.

The Amashina requested several of their larger whale-like allies to accompany them. While Flash hadn't heard of an animal like the one Diego described in his nightmare, he admitted there were creatures inhabiting the depths unknown to them.

When the group settled on board, the robot started the boat, which ran on a silent type of engine. It had enough power to speed across the water. Diego hoped the group hadn't left the Amashina too far behind. Then Frake leaped out of the water. So much for worrying about leaving his friends behind. The spouting breath of other creatures appeared farther out. It took half of the morning to reach the place Feelona thought they should explore. The boat slowed, then stopped, and the Amashina gathered around.

"We will feed for a short while and then we can swim down to the bottom," she said, her squeaks punctuating the words in his communicator.

Diego nodded and gathered his weapon. He bypassed the ladder and swung over the railing, splashing feet first into the deep green waters. Rreengrol and the two Turengens followed. As before, Jeng and Fress swam in loops and spirals in their joy at being back in the water. Diego swam around the boat, getting used to the water again.

He watched their surroundings but didn't gawk as he had before. Schools of vividly colored fish parted for them as they swam deeper and deeper. They followed the slope of an underwater escarpment. Plant-like animals on the rocks folded their flowers, which disappeared into plain tubes resembling flower stalks. Crabs of various odd shapes and sizes scuttled along the rocks as the group continued deeper.

So far, Diego had not felt discomfort other than a slight chill. Then, they crossed into an area where the bottom was less populated. A few eel-like creatures scurried across the open area but nothing else. They continued further, using their suit lights to see what was ahead. Even those only lit a short distance, perhaps only the length of two horses or two reops like his friend Fuerte. Diego stared into the shadows, trying to see if anything lurked there. His dream continued to flash into his mind, making him more wary.

A creature that resembled a shark with a sail-like tail and glowing eyes meandered out of the dark, opening its enormous mouth and shaking its head. The teeth glowed, too. It backed away as fast as it had shown itself.

"The suits have a repellent—a very low sub-sonic signal that most large creatures don't like," Flash explained. He swam close to Diego and then spiraled around to the other side of the group.

We are ready for any creatures. I think.... Jeng sent into his mind.

Diego had to chuckle at that one. His suit provided fresh water, and he drank a few swallows of it. Despite being in and surrounded by water, he knew he had to stay hydrated while they swam. Several large fish, as wide as they were long, swam into view, their long noses flashing with rosy colored light. They turned and swam away when they saw the size of the approaching group. Diego shivered in the cold of the deep waters and then felt the suit heat a few degrees.

They approached the sides of an ocean shelf. He spied more life here, but the fish stayed close to waving sea plants, the rocks, and corals growing on the rocks. Diego felt a chill having nothing to do with the suit and tried to gaze deeper into the inky blackness ahead of him. The ground shook. Another seaquake? But the Trologs were gone.

No, everything around them quivered and shook—water, ocean floor, and fish. Huge tentacles rose from below them. The plants flattened to the ground, and the fish fled. An underwater laser blast shot toward it, even as Diego saw the largest tentacle reaching toward him. Then he had a flash of realization—this wasn't something that he could change, but a future happening.

"Don't kill it. It's going to show us the Trolog artifacts!" he shouted into his communicator.

The tentacle wrapped around him and pulled him closer to the creature. Another grabbed at one of the Amashina, but they shot out of its grasp. It snatched Jeng instead. The Turengen chittered his fear, but he didn't fight back. The creature dragged them away from the group. Someone fired another laser shot.

"Diego!" Rreengrol shouted in his helmet. "We'll try to disable it!"

"Stop shooting!" Diego called. "Just follow." He kept a tight grip on his own rifle, a hard task as the tentacle squeezed against his ribcage. He took shallow breaths. It grew harder and harder, and he felt the incredible speed of the unseen creature as it withdrew from the group. The pressure increased, and Diego worried about losing consciousness. Then, the tentacle drew him through the hole he had seen in his dream. The tentacle with Jeng followed.

That hadn't been in his dream; at least, he didn't remember anyone else being captured. The tentacle continued drawing them through the cylinder. Diego only saw dim shadows as it jerked him back. Listless plants grew on metal; tiny gray fish darted out of the way.

In the light of his helmet light, Diego saw a gigantic mouth with scimitar-like teeth and glowing eyes—six of them. The creature drew Jeng closer to its mouth. It planned on eating him!

"Jeng, if you…can get a clear shot—fire!" Despite having his breath almost squeezed out of his body, Diego raised the weapon and fired it. The light blinded him as he fired a second shot. The creature roared when the blasts hit it in the face. Both shots scored and more weapons fired from behind him. The creature sped backward again at a speed that astonished Diego. Soon, he and Jeng were alone with the monster. Again, the tentacle drew Jeng closer to the sharp teeth.

"Jeng!" Diego called out. He heard other voices coming through the communicator, but they seemed faint. The tentacle holding him tight squeezed harder. He raised his weapon again, groaning at the pain in his chest.

CHAPTER TWENTY-FIVE

He fired. Diego felt the crack of something in his chest—intense pain—and then the tentacle released him. It whipped back toward the terrifying face. Diego fired again, even as a sharp stab of pain messed up his aim. The laser scored along the top of the monster's head and into the darkness beyond. It screamed, and the tentacles flailed out like whips. The tip snapped against his weapon, jerking it out of his hand. Jeng fired. This time, the creature squealed, so high-pitched it hurt Diego's ears. He found the control for his headlamp, raising the power, and the immediate area grew brighter.

This creature was worse than any nightmare. It looked like a bloated spider with tentacles rather than legs. Thick, dark fluid leaked from several places behind its head and torso.

"Jeng?" he gasped. "Feelona?" The pain still lingered but dulled to a throbbing ache. "Jeng?" Diego looked around for the Turengen even while the tentacles drifted to the bottom of the cylinder.

"Here...." The weak sound of the Turengen's voice told Diego that Jeng was injured. "Where are you?"

"Near monster."

Diego tried to swim closer to the dying creature, but his chest was on fire. He held one arm tight against his ribs and paddled with his other. That was better, but it still hurt. Finally, the monster stopped moving, and Diego drew closer. His light showed a smaller mound ahead of him. He drifted toward the bottom of the cylinder and shuffled forward. Jeng lay a few feet in front of the monster. Diego reached him and kneeled beside the Turengen. "Jeng?"

"Side hurts," he moaned.

"Can you contact Fress?"

"Can't...."

"That's all right. Feelona, Rreengrol, can you hear me?"

He heard static and then a scratchy voice. "Diego?"

"We're inside the cylinder. I have my light on bright."

"Can't find where you went." That was Rreengrol. "Wait. I see your light now!"

Diego saw light bobbing some distance away. Had that thing dragged them so far? "I see someone. With a light." Diego bit back a moan. He knew Jeng was even worse off. "We both have injuries."

Then Flash swam in front of him. He checked out the monster. "The creature is dead." He drew closer to Diego but didn't touch his chest. "We will take you and the Turengen to the medical facilities."

"Don't lose this place. I think this is what Treela was talking about. The lost Trolog artifacts."

We'll explore this later, but we need to get you both to the surface and then the facility.

"Yes."

"There is a piece of fabric on your suit. One on each shoulder."

Diego reached up with one arm and found what Flash was talking about. He tugged, and the fabric released from his suit and floated out in front of him. It resembled a harness. They were going to pull him through the ocean. "Get Jeng first. I think he's worse."

"We will pull you out, then Frake will have room to get Jeng."

Diego couldn't argue. The heat inside the suit had increased, helping him to relax. He felt the shadows creeping around the edges of his consciousness. There was a gentle tug, and he felt himself being pulled out of the Trolog artifact.

Rreengrol swam into his line of vision. "We're taking you to the surface, but it will take a little while. Just hang on."

Diego saw the humor of the pun. "What else would I do?" Then he remembered Jeng. "Wait for Jeng."

"No, Commander. Fress and other Amashina will take care of Jeng. Flash and I are taking you topside."

"Okay." Those shadows around the edge of his mind deepened, and Diego remembered little of the trip. He knew the Amashina traded off a few times before they reached the boat. Rreengrol and the robot helped him aboard. His friend sat beside him. Then Diego observed Fress and Rreengrol lifting Jeng on board. The robot took its place at the bow and started up the engine. As the boat skimmed across the waves, the Amashina leaped in and out of the bow waves. The sun dipped below the horizon as they returned to the spaceport. Diego watched the stars come out, and tried to count meteors to stay awake. One large meteor grew larger and larger before he realized his eyes were out of focus. Diego blinked and looked over at Jeng. The Turengen was still, and Diego couldn't tell if he was alive or dead.

The medical robots were waiting at the ramp. That was the last thing Diego remembered.

CHAPTER TWENTY-SIX

Diego woke up in the medical bay. His side ached, but there was little pain. "Jeng!" Diego looked around and saw his entire crew nearby. The two Turengens stood near Jeng's bed, and Rreengrol, Treela, and Rrishan were close to his bed. The robot medical staff made tinny complaints every time they had to move around the bay.

"I feel better." Diego drew in a deep breath. The pain didn't increase. He figured the robots used something like the device applied to him when they had fought the Koressians.

"You had several broken ribs, one of which damaged a lung," the nearest robot said, realizing he was awake. "We have been able to take care of your lungs, and your ribs are almost healed, but you will rest for the next few days. There is only so much our healing device can do in such a short time."

"What?" Diego cried, thinking of all the time wasted instead of exploring the artifacts.

"Those are our orders, and the Amashina will honor them. You will come back here to receive further treatment until we release you from medical care. Those orders apply to the young Turengen as well. If you comply, you can recuperate and rest in your quarters."

Rreengrol shrugged. "You heard the command, Commander."

Diego couldn't help it. Despite his frustration, he grinned. "How long have I been in here?"

"This is the second day the sun has risen over your sleeping body."

"Santa Maria!" he cried. "What have I missed?"

"Jeng is going to be all right, and Marix Ziron called once, asking that you return his communication as soon as you were well enough."

"I would much prefer to make the call in our guest room."

"I figured." Rreengrol held up a ship's leisure suit.

Diego realized he was almost naked under his blanket. "Thanks, Rreengrol. If you all will leave, I'll get dressed and return to our quarters."

"I will bring breakfast to your suite," the robot intoned.

Diego could almost swear he heard relief in the robot's voice. Rreengrol laughed, but they all filed out. Diego slid on the comfortable clothes and felt his ribs.

"You are to do nothing strenuous," the robot reminded him. "And your healing will be quicker if you return daily for healing sessions."

Diego checked Jeng, who was waking up. "How are you feeling?"

Jeng felt up and down his body and then chittered, his tone upbeat in happiness. "Better, Commander."

"Seressin devices make life better. The robots said we could finish recuperating in our rooms."

Jeng sat up. "Good! I am ready to go."

Diego waited for the Turengen, and they walked out together. The others were waiting.

"So, what did you find down there?" Treela asked. "Besides a gigantic monster."

"We can explain during breakfast if you can wait that long," Diego said.

He first contacted Marix Ziron in his room.

"You are healing?" the Seressin asked.

"Yes, Marix. The facilities are excellent."

Ziron nodded. "I have sent out a medium battlecruiser to the Amashi system to provide protection in case the Trologs invade."

Diego couldn't judge if that would deter Trologs or not. "I was told our ship's repairs will be completed within a short time. Bress didn't get specific or have a distinct timeline, sir. He is supervising the work."

"Did you find anything down there in the ocean?"

"Only a sea monster living inside an unknown and unnatural artifact. I assumed it was Trolog. The Amashina didn't recognize it. As soon as I am cleared to go back, we are swimming down to the cylinder and exploring thoroughly."

"Keep me apprised of what you discover, Commander."

"Yes, sir, Marix!"

Again, the Seressin cut the connection. Diego joined the others in the common area.

"Is Marix Ziron pleased with the discovery?" Rrishan asked.

Diego sat down at the low table, covered with dishes of food. "As far as I know, but I think he'll be even happier when we find artifacts."

Diego took a bite or two from each dish. The Amashi meals hadn't disappointed him yet.

Treela looked up from her plate. "How did the Amashina know where to look? Father didn't even have an idea."

"The Amashina keep their records by relating them verbally from one generation to another. Like a storyteller," Diego explained. "After they listened to the old stories of your people's colonization, the leaders had a vague idea where a Trolog city might have sunk. We didn't have to explore at all. The Amashina had it figured out. Of course, their remembrance was of an enormous explosion, one so powerful that it blew away the land mass. So, this cylinder could have been somewhere else at one time."

"And the creature is dead?"

"As far as we know," Diego replied.

Treela had used some Seressin words. Diego realized she had a gift for languages, just as he did.

"I'd like to go back with you."

"If the Amashina can make suits for us in such a short time, I can't imagine them not being able to make you one. Rreengrol, could you find out?"

"Of course!" He gazed at Treela. "Do you swim on your home planet?"

"Yes, I know how to swim. We have underground lakes."

Diego smiled. "You'll like this swim."

"As long as oversized sea monsters don't eat me, Commander."

"Please call me Diego."

Treela nodded, a smile on her face.

"I'll go talk to the Amashina about a suit." Rreengrol got up.

Diego thanked his friend and then turned back to Treela. "Do you know what your father was looking for?"

"First, he wanted proof our people had been here, then...." She paused. "He was looking for something to prove the creatures here destroyed them." Again, she paused. "Centuries-old rumors claim the scientists here developed a weapon."

"Maybe that's what destroyed them," Diego suggested.

"I don't know. Maybe what we find will answer all our questions."

"That's a possibility." Diego continued his meal.

They both sat without speaking for several moments. Diego noticed the others had finished and gone elsewhere. He and Treela were alone.

Apparently, she noticed it as well. "I would like to go out on the balcony and watch the ocean. Could you come with me?"

The clouds were golden in the mid-morning sun and

danced across the blue-green sky like colts. He thought of Fuerte, then Tejas. It was easier to picture the reop than the horse he had raised from a colt. That brought a pang of guilt as though he had abandoned his friend. Of course, Tejas was dead, killed by the very people he admired and worked with. Diego let it go. This was his world now, however he got here.

"The Seressin are slaveholders, aren't they?"

Diego turned his attention to Treela. "Yes, but it's changing."

"Because of you."

Diego shook his head. "No, because the Seressin and their allies are changing."

"Because of you. You were a slave. Why are you so loyal to the person who enslaved you?"

Diego wondered who had told her that. "He put me in a position that allowed me to overcome my station. I refused to remain a slave and was willing to do anything to gain freedom. Marix Ziron not only freed me, but the Turengens as well. And other creatures."

"What about Rreengrol and Rrishan?"

"No, the Grrlocks formed an alliance several generations ago, but they were also advancing in the military hierarchy when the Seressin captured me. And now there are female applicants to warrior positions on Seressin warships." Diego wondered why he was opening up so much, but he pushed that question away. Treela was the first human he'd seen in almost two years. Or as close to his species as possible. He remembered Ziron's warning and then pushed it aside, too.

"We have had slavery on Trolog. Still do in some places. I think it's reprehensible."

"I didn't like it much myself," Diego said with a smile. "When I get my battleship, I plan on manning it with volunteers."

"Even the nasty jobs?" she asked, returning his smile.

"Perhaps offer freedom in exchange for working nasty jobs. Or good pay." He frowned. "How about changing the subject to more pleasant things, like what do you think we'll find down there?"

Treela grew thoughtful. "Hopefully, not dead bodies."

"Not after this long, I would guess."

"You're right." She nodded. "Perhaps bowls and spoons and baby beds?"

Diego looked askance at her. "Or gold coins and swords."

"What?"

Diego laughed. "That was the object for those crazy enough to look for treasures on sunken ships on my world. No one had special suits like here."

"Are we crazy?" she asked.

"Probably, but not too crazy."

She looked up. "That cloud looks like a very fluffy pranlis."

"Pranlis?"

"It has long fur that curls at the end, and a tail like Rrishan's, and four legs. Its ears are on top of its head and kind of round. Its eyes are a very dark blue."

Diego thought he knew what the pranlis was. "Does it have?" and he made a motion of whiskers coming out from the side of its face.

"Yes. They are short but very thick."

"A cat."

"A what?"

"I think your pranlis is like a cat on my world. The Grrlocks are cat-like."

"I had one before I made this trip. He was old, and I don't think he will be alive when I get back home." Treela sighed.

"I'm sorry."

They were quiet again. Diego thought about the girl standing next to him.

CHAPTER TWENTY-SEVEN

The promised starship, *Black Star,* cruised near the gate, a young Seressin commander at the helm. Diego felt better knowing that Amashi was protected.

Treela modeled her new exploration suit to the group. She insisted on choosing the colors, so hers ended up different from the ones created for Diego's crew. It was silver with blue highlights down the side.

"Why that color scheme?" Rrishan asked, sounding jealous. Their blue suits had no highlights.

"I've always liked metallic colors," Treela answered. "When do we go out?"

The group went out to explore the ancient wreckage the next day. Diego was eager but apprehensive. Bress stayed behind, as did Jeng, to work on their ship. Rrishan and Treela would join them, so with the Amashina there would be a large group.

Puffy, golden-tinged gray clouds gathered the next morning, hinting at rain later in the day. The same ship that took them out before took them to the site of the artifact, and they began the long swim down. Half a dozen Amashina accompanied them. Diego brought an undersea rifle, as well as a recorder, in case they couldn't take what they found to the surface. The others had similar weapons. Rrishan and Treela also carried small recorders. Diego watched Treela swim with a powerful, rhythmic kick.

He pulled his gaze away. *There could be other monsters down here, and I need to stay focused.* He turned on his light at the low setting and spied Amashina in front and on each side of their group. Fress swam close to him but didn't do more than wave, and then she darted closer to Treela. Rrishan also caught up with

Treela, her swimming much surer.

As they drew closer to the cylinder, Diego felt the ominous presence of the creature that lived there for so long. He kept telling himself they had killed it, but it didn't make him less nervous.

"Are you all right, Commander?" Feelona asked as she swam close. Her sinuous dolphin-like body moved in a cadenced motion, with the tail fluke doing most of the work. The Amashina's long-fingered fins stayed close to her body unless she needed to change direction or to stay in place.

"I am doing well, thank you, Leader."

"Do you wish to go in with the first group as you did before?"

"Yes, I would."

"Only three or four individuals can enter at a time. As you know, the entrance to the cylinder is small. I would like to accompany you."

"It would be an honor. I will alert my crew and choose two others to go with us." Diego swam toward Treela and the others. "Treela?"

She turned toward him and smiled.

Diego returned the smile. "You, Feelona, Fress, and I are going in first. Then Rreengrol, Rrishan, and two other Amashina after we get inside."

"It feels scary down here. Are we close?" Rrishan asked.

"Yes, very close," Diego replied. "This is pretty near to where the monster grabbed Jeng and me."

"Do you think Jeng didn't come because of what the monster did to him?" Treela asked.

Diego frowned. "No. Bress asked for Jeng's help with the ship." Diego swam ahead, a bit disturbed by her question and not understanding why.

The entrance to the cylinder loomed ahead, and Diego backpedaled to slow down. Feelona swam beside him. "Frake already went inside a short time ago and reports no other creatures like the one that attacked you and the Turengen."

"Good, let's go in." Diego kicked toward the hole before his determination wavered. Despite the Amashina's reassurance, his mind conjured up creatures slipping out of the shadows. He turned his light up to show more of the artifact.

Treela followed close behind, then Feelona and Fress. Diego only heard the movement of the sickly-looking plants swaying inside the cylinder. He continued and came to the place where they had killed the creature. A small school of fist-sized fish, silvery in the light, scavenged along the floor of the structure.

Diego swam further into the cylinder, finding rocks stacked in peculiar formations, along with bones and dead plants. The tube continued in places caved in, but otherwise, the same dimensions the further they went. They came across the spot where someone had connected another tube to the main one. The size was the same. They found the end crumpled and blocked with rocks and boulders after swimming a short distance.

The group returned to the main cylinder and continued, Feelona swimming ahead. Treela followed close behind. Diego ended up at the end of the exploration party, but it didn't bother him. His light lit up dark corners where battered refuse lay. He dug into different piles, finding remains of the sea monster's meals, but sometimes, he found unusual pieces of metal or other materials—like some of the lightweight materials found on starship control panels.

He stuffed those in the specimen bag at his waist. Several ropy black plants or animals hung almost in his face. Diego looked up to see Flash swimming up beside him.

"What are you seeing?" the Amashina asked.

"Does it look like there might be little doors or, uh, cabinets with covers?"

"If we can convince the creatures to let us look, we'll see."

"Are they dangerous?"

"If disturbed, they could be dangerous. They appear to be a variant of a species of animal I am familiar with."

Diego brightened his light as high as it would go, and the rope animals pulled back. "I'm going to reach beyond them. There is something there."

"Be careful, Commander. I will shine my extra light."

"Thanks." Diego reached between the tendrils and found a small, round door. He tugged. At first, it didn't want to open. Diego pried with his spear-like tool, and the door broke. A puff of debris sprinkled down on them. The nearby animals hissed like cats but kept back. Small items fell onto the cylinder floor. Diego used his spear to check for anything else.

Diego found more doors, some larger, some of different shapes. The ropy creatures grew bolder, and Diego had to shoot one trying to grab him. The others held back. He opened all the doors and then he, Fress, and Treela gathered up everything falling out of the small cabinets. Diego didn't check what he had picked up. If it didn't bite him, it ended up in the specimen bag.

He continued through the cylinder ahead of the others, not finding any more of the storage units. Another cylinder branched out from the main one. Flash, Rreengrol, and Rrishan caught up with him. They paddled into the new corridor, then stopped.

Before them was a darkness his light couldn't penetrate. Diego tried to turn the headlamp brighter, but it couldn't penetrate the shadow. A tiny fish swam ahead of them. Then it disappeared.

"What is that?" Rreengrol said.

Diego wanted to say 'Hell,' but he didn't. It appeared the darkness swallowed up any light or creature coming close. He examined the floor of the smaller cylinder. Rocks littered the area. He collected a few metallic pieces to examine later. Diego kept one eye on the dark circle and one on their surroundings.

He picked up a rock and threw it toward the dark void. The rock disappeared. There was no clunk of it hitting anything. It just disappeared like something going into the gates between stars. Flashes appeared on the edges of the murky circle, and then they vanished as well. "A black hole? A gate?" Water swirled past them and into the blackness.

"It's scary," Rrishan said.

The water swirled harder, and Diego felt as though it drew him toward the blackness. The rocks by his feet slid closer to it and then pieces of the ceiling. Diego felt Rreengrol grabbing the back of his suit and pulling him away. The water sluiced past him as they continued to draw back. They finally reached the main corridor.

Then it all stopped — the water, the rocks, the crumpled metal, even the darkness deeper than regular darkness. Diego's light shone on a dark circle, but it appeared small and benign. Nothing like the sucking, powerful entity of just a few seconds ago. Where in the world could it have gone — whatever it was?

Rreengrol's voice shook as he asked some of the same things Diego wondered. "Is that a black hole? Or a stellar portal? At the bottom of the ocean?"

"But if it is a black hole, why hasn't it sucked up everything in the ocean?" Diego asked. "And why and how did it stop?"

"It didn't seem to do anything until we came," Flash added, his fingers twitching. "I need to tell the others." He left almost before his last words echoed in Diego's helmet.

Diego considered Flash's words. Then he stepped forward, his flippered feet just inside the side corridor. The darkness widened, and water swirled past him with small flashes around the edges.

"What are you doing?" Rreengrol hissed.

Diego backpedaled into the main corridor. "Just curious. I think we activated it."

"Curiosity isn't a good thing right now," Rreengrol added. Diego agreed. His skin crawled.

"It seems kind of evil to me," Rrishan said.

"I think so, too." Diego paused in thought. "I don't think we need to let others know what this thing does, except the Leadership. I'm not sure I should report this to Marix Ziron." Rreengrol's eyes widened. "At least not now."

"Why?" Rreengrol asked.

"Do you realize if this thing is a gate, what kind of weapon it would make? And how many others might want it? Especially if someone could duplicate it. Imagine a gate directly from Resh to Seressin."

Rreengrol remained silent for some time. "Maybe you're right."

They heard the noise of the others swimming down the corridor. Feelona hovered near Diego's side. "Your discovery agitated Flash. What is it?"

"It seems to be something similar to black holes existing in space," Diego said.

Feelona waved all her tentacles. "What is its purpose?"

"I don't know," Diego said.

Treela's cry echoed in his helmet. She pushed forward, past the Amashina, past Rreengrol. Fress was right behind her. Her forward momentum shoved her into Diego, who half-swam, half-fell into the corridor. The darkness deepened, and the water swirled again. Treela swam past him, seemingly mesmerized by the blackness before her.

Rreengrol tried to grab her but caught onto Diego instead. Fress chittered.

Treela kept swimming. "Something my ancestors made!"

"Come back, Treela," Diego shouted. She ignored him, swimming toward the swirling water, pebbles, sand, and debris.

He grabbed her leg. Rrishan reached for Diego's belt. "Get

back, Rrishan! That's an order!" Rrishan let go.

Treela reached the blackness and disappeared into it. Diego kept hold of her ankle and felt like his body was being stretched and then jerked apart. Heat seared his mind, and cold enveloped his body. He screwed his eyes shut. Something screamed inside his helmet — other voices of agony joined the screaming. Diego wanted to let go of Treela and cover his ears, but he couldn't. He couldn't bear to be alone in whatever hell he inhabited now.

Diego fell against something hard. Ground? He opened his eyes and saw more blackness. He felt his body rising. Floating. Was he floating? He had been in the ocean. Was he still there? Diego blinked and saw a bit of light around the fringes of his eyes — flashes of light showing him nothing. He continued floating, but his mind shut down. Diego remembered nothing else.

CHAPTER TWENTY-EIGHT

Diego opened his eyes and then snapped them shut. The glare was painful. And so hot—even in the water. His body banged against something hard with every wave. An object bumped against his chest. When his eyes adjusted to the brightness, Diego raised his head and studied his surroundings. His back lay against a craggy rock, and Rreengrol floated in front of him. There was a narrow, rocky beach, but the water they lay in was murky, with dead plants and an oily film floating on the surface.

He crawled farther up on land, dragging Rreengrol with him. Diego's muscles seemed to have turned into mush, so his progress was in inches rather than feet. He reached beyond the waves and collapsed on the beach, panting for breath. An odd smell permeated the air he was breathing. He coughed, hoping it didn't worsen.

Gazing up the beach, Diego saw a small mound about ten feet away. Fress! Diego staggered to his feet. He left Rreengrol and checked out the Turengen. Her chest rose and fell, filling him with relief. Then he checked Rreengrol, who groaned. Where had Treela disappeared to? He searched for footprints, but the muck on shore made them impossible to find. "Rreengrol! Rreengrol! Wake up."

"What?" Rreengrol tried to sit up. Diego helped him. "Where are we?"

"I guess this is where the black hole dumped us."

"What was Treela thinking?" he groaned.

"I don't even know where she is right now, but Fress came through with us."

Rreengrol blinked and started taking his helmet off.

Diego stopped him. "I don't know what the atmosphere is like. It has a nasty smell." He looked up and shuddered at the reddish-brown cast to the sky. Then, he studied the various warnings flickering across the front of his helmet. All he needed to do to read them was raise his eyes just above the clear front of the face mask. Normally, the symbols shone in light blue, telling him all was well. Now angry red and yellow letters shouted the foul condition of the air. Residual messages reassured him that the mask had protected him from pollutants in the water, too.

"Where are we?" Rreengrol repeated, pushing himself up from the gray sand. "Oh, yeah, on the other side of the portal. Oh, what a mess! My tail hurts, and I can't even get out of this suit to stretch it."

Diego ignored Rreengrol. "When Fress wakes up and is able, we'll try to find Treela. Somehow, she ended up better than we did.

Rreengrol waved his hand toward the waves and their sickly residue. "Glad these suits come with some sustenance pouches. I wouldn't want to eat any of this."

"I agree." How were they going to get back? Was there something on this end to pull them back to Amashi? He hoped so. First, they had to find Treela. Then, they could reconnoiter and find shelter.

Diego gazed into the brown-tinted sky. The sun was a huge red ball, at least twice the size of the sun on his home world. In some parts of the sky, the haze thickened into gray clouds, the red tinge making them seem angry. Wind swirled around them, picking up grit and peppering them with it.

"Fress," Diego called softly. "Wake up."

Soft chittering told him the Turengen was regaining consciousness. She rolled over and tried to sit up.

Diego helped her. "Are you hurt?"

Fish guts and muck worms! She made a few other mental

comments, but they were not understandable. Diego figured that was just as well.

Rreengrol must have heard her because he chuckled. "Commander...."

"Diego," he told his second in command. "Don't start getting formal on me now. There is nothing to command."

"Well, okay, Diego. We would feel better if we could find some shade."

"You're right. I'll look around."

"Did our weapons come with us? I don't see mine."

Something had ripped away the laser gun from Diego's waist, holster included, but he found his knife still in its sheath. He looked in the pocket on his thigh and found a small laser pistol. Fress found hers. Rreengrol dug out his little palm-sized pistol.

"Better than nothing," the Grrlock admitted.

"We'll need to be sparing with them so they last until we can get back home."

Fress got to her feet. *Where is Treela?*

"When I came to, she was gone, and I couldn't find any footprints," Diego replied.

She seemed happy when we got to this side of the portal. I felt only a brief flash from her mind before I passed out.

I wonder why?

Maybe this is a place she knows?

Trolog, Diego ventured. He remembered her comment about her ancestors.

Fress gazed at him but didn't answer.

"Let's get moving. I don't think we're going to accomplish anything sitting here and roasting under this sun." Diego clipped his fins to his belt.

Rreengrol groaned as he straightened up, but they were soon walking up the beach to a ridge of boulders standing sentinel over the murky brown water. To one side rose a rocky cliff. It appeared pockmarked with places to get out of the sun and wind, but the threesome had no strength to climb. He continued toward the rocky boundary.

The land continued upward, but now they were walking on rocky soil rather than sand. Then everything leveled out. The wind pulled at them. The haze made everything fuzzy, but Diego thought he saw some kind of building in the distance. Would the inhabitants be friendly? He saw no sign of Treela.

"Are those buildings?" Rreengrol asked.

"I think so. Fress, are you feeling any thoughts from anyone?"

"No. I hear nothing but the wind."

"A rather desolate place." Diego studied their surroundings. "I am not sure how long it will be before the sun sets. We don't need to walk toward unknown buildings with unknown inhabitants. We need to spy on them and see what they're like."

Fress pointed toward the rock formations. "Rest in the lee of the boulders?"

"Yes."

They found a place where all three could sit in the shadows. It also kept the wind-borne sand from peppering them.

Rreengrol sighed. "I'm just glad Rrishan didn't get pulled into this."

"I am, too. As well as the Amashina."

"They could not survive here," Fress pointed out.

No one said anything, which suited Diego fine. He didn't want to think about being stranded in this place.

Thankfully, the sun soon set behind the rocks. A deep dryness seeped inside his suit. Diego watched a strange-looking insect scuttle across the ground in front of them. It stopped twice, balancing on two legs. The beetle had an extra body part — making it not as long as a centipede but longer than a beetle. Diego also noticed seven legs, one pushing it along from the rear. The dirt exploded, and something snatched the insect, dragging it back into the ground before Diego could blink.

"I hope it only likes bugs," Rreengrol whispered. "Whatever it is."

Fress sat on Diego's right. "I think we should see if there is any way back through the portal."

Diego didn't answer for a moment. He thought about Treela and leaving her behind if they found a way back. Of course, she left them behind, another sign this was her home. If so, then he accomplished part of his goal by returning her back home. Still, he felt they needed to find Treela. He wondered if they should split up, and he could find the girl while the other two checked out the portal.

No!

Diego gazed at the dust devils in the distance where the sun still shone. "What is your reasoning, Fress?"

"We are already split up, Commander. We do not need to split up more in this place." Fress made a soft chittering cough. "And my apologies for infringing."

"No, it's all right. Is it also your belief this is Treela's home world?"

"Many things point to it."

"Wouldn't her abandonment of us be another point?" Rreengrol reasoned.

Diego knew they were right. "All right. We've rested, and the daylight is fading. If we're going back into the water to check it out, it needs to be soon. I don't even know how long we were in this ocean before we washed ashore."

"Don't think it's too far from shore." Fress got up and stretched.

"And how are we going to figure out where we entered

this place?" Diego asked.

Fress chittered. "Not sure, but we must check."

CHAPTER TWENTY-NINE

By the time the trio reached the water, the large sun had slid below the edge of the horizon. Diego saw why Fress figured their entrance to this world was close to the shoreline. This wasn't an ocean. He could see the far shore and jagged mountains. "This is a large lake rather than an ocean." Diego stepped over lines of washed-up sludge and continued walking into the water. He waited until he was all the way in before he pulled on his fins. Despite the difficulty, he finally achieved the task. The others were waiting for him, their lights on.

The lake appeared to be dead, but Diego kept his hand near his knife. By silent consensus, they swam toward the deepest part. He observed a small worm-like creature undulating below him. It snapped its tiny jaws on something even tinier floating nearby. Diego saw several more as they swam deeper.

Finally, Rreengrol reached the rocky bottom, almost running into a boulder in the murkiness. "Can't believe how nasty this is."

"Let's spread out in a pattern and see if we find anything," Diego suggested. "Not too far away from each other."

The group swam hand-tip to hand-tip, occasionally feeling the contours of the lake bottom. As the darkness deepened, they continued until the suits blared warnings. Red breathing level warnings were bright enough to hurt Diego's eyes. There was a raw taste in his mouth, and his lungs felt as clogged as the surrounding water. "Return to shore," he ordered.

"I see a glint ahead of us." Rreengrol pointed and then coughed.

Diego followed the Grrlock, seeing the same glint.

Rreengrol reached under the silt and pulled up an undersea laser rifle. "This is mine. It came through when we did."

They searched for more weapons but found none. "We'll take whatever luck we can get and be happy with it," Diego commented. They swam slowly, conserving energy.

The trio crawled out of the lake, collapsing on the rocky shore. A few stars glittered their dim light at them. Diego saw no moon. A scream pierced the darkness. Diego couldn't tell if it was a bird or some land animal.

"Someone comes," Fress announced.

Diego sat up. "Which direction?" The foul air still irritated his throat.

"From beyond the boulders. I think from the building we saw in the distance."

The darkness kept them from searching for a place to hide. "We wait. Be ready."

Rreengrol coughed. "I wish we could clean out the oxygen exchangers in our suits."

Diego gazed at the read-outs and saw the suit was doing some cleaning, just not enough. He rose to his feet and stumbled closer to the boundary of rocks. Leaning against one, he peered toward the slope and detected several bobbing lights heading in their direction. Diego continued his surveillance, trying to use their own lights to see what weapons they had.

They took their time but went unerringly toward the spot where the group had come ashore earlier. Diego watched them, counting six figures. If they had to fight, it would be two to one. He hoped it wouldn't come to that.

The animal screamed again, a little closer this time but still distant. There was a slight noise coming from the cliff to his right. The sound was like nails scraping on the rocks. And it came closer.

"Fress," he hissed. There was no answer. Diego felt a stir

of panic. Was the Turengen all right? "Rreengrol?"

"Hmm?"

"There's an animal crawling around above us."

Diego moved away, slowing when he tripped over a jutting rock in the dark. He turned his light toward the noise.

Climbing down the rock was something resembling a centipede, only many times larger and with the girth of a good-sized steer. Its head swung from side to side, not liking the light. Tooth-like mandibles grew out of the sides of the mouth, clacking together. It hissed and screeched. Diego had his small laser ready and fired at the creature. His aim was excellent, and he hit it square on the head, just above the mouth. The upper body thrashed, but it kept coming. He fired again, this time behind its pumpkin-sized bulbous head. It flailed up toward the sky, and its front legs let go of the rock. Diego shot one more time, hitting the animal's underside. The creature screeched and fell off the cliff, hitting the ground with enough force to shake the earth. It hissed, then curled up and was still.

Rreengrol and Fress stumbled closer to the dead animal, their weapons out.

"Fress, are you all right?"

"Yes. I heard you. Low on oxygen. Hard to talk."

"I think I was, too," Rreengrol mumbled.

"Be careful," Diego warned.

Another light shone on the giant centipede. Diego jerked around, his hand shielding his eyes.

The slight click of a machine preceded speech in another language. "Put your hand down and then throw your weapon toward us."

"Get your light out of my eyes, and I might follow your instructions," snapped Diego. After a moment, the light lowered to chest level, and he dropped his weapon.

"And the others. Weapons to the ground."

"Go ahead." *Not the hidden weapons.*

"Diego!" a voice called out.

He wasn't totally surprised. "Treela? Are you all right?"

"Of course. You're all right now, too."

Diego turned to the Trolog, the one giving all the directions. "If there are more of these creatures, I would like the ability to protect myself." He pointed at his weapon.

"No need to worry about that."

Treela reached out and touched him on the arm. "Don't worry, Diego."

"Come with us," the voice ordered.

Diego lowered the light level on his visor. He didn't know how long the suit could maintain the self-containment systems, and they might need them later.

Treela picked up their weapons and then fell in step beside them. "That's the biggest crazzworm I've ever seen. You are good luck for us to bring in one so big."

"Bring in?"

"Their meat is wonderful, especially marinated in friscan wine."

"So, you hunt those things for food?"

"Our people hunt anything for food."

"I assume this is Trolog?"

"Yes. I know it's not as pretty as Amashi, but some areas are nice."

"Did you know about that portal we found in the ocean?"

"No. There were legends about such doorways, but I didn't think it was possible until I saw it. Did you try to find this side of it?"

"Yes."

"And you didn't find it."

"No."

"Too bad."

Diego said nothing for a moment. "Did you want to go back to Amashi?"

"I wanted to find artifacts, so the doorway would have been an easy way to come back home."

Diego thought of the pouch he filled with the various Trolog materials. He wondered if they had any kind of value. Of course, if their captors searched them, it wouldn't matter.

Perhaps we should find a place to hide them before we get to these people's home, Fress suggested.

If we can.

Treela cocked her head to the side. "By the way, why do you still have your helmets on?"

"Because we were getting warnings about the air. We weren't getting enough oxygen."

"Are you now?" Treela asked.

Diego checked the warnings and saw there were none. He also noticed the wind had calmed, and the temperature had dropped. "Interesting. Why is the air cleaner at night?"

"Always has been. Father said it was the wind blowing around all the pollutants during the day, making it hard to breathe."

"He's right. How long has it been like this?"

"For hundreds of cycles. Not every place is this bad, though. We're near the equator, but it's getting harder to live here."

"You are talking too much. Save your breath for walking," the gravelly voiced leader ordered.

"We're friends. Diego helped me get home."

"And I am the leader of this operation, so no more talking."

Treela muttered, but Diego couldn't understand. She continued walking next to them while Diego tried figuring out her actual status with these people. She didn't seem to be in as much trouble as she said she would. Then he wondered about their own status.

The light showed puffs of dust rising at their footfalls. Diego saw more lights approaching and heard the noise of a machine. A ride?

The vehicle slowed as it approached them and then continued toward the lake.

Treela explained. "The meat recovery vehicle. That crazzworm is too valuable to leave to scavengers."

The leader growled, and Treela grew silent again.

I think we are prisoners.

Diego figured Fress was right.

CHAPTER THIRTY

Just before arriving at the tallest building, Fress stumbled and fell. Diego was by her side in an instant. *Here, we can deposit our specimen bags.* Rreengrol was by her other side and his smaller bag ended up in the hole next to hers and then Diego's. It amazed him she had even seen this in the dark. She pushed several fist-sized rocks against them. Diego could only hope the bags would remain hidden.

"Not that far a walk!" the leader barked. "Back on your feet!"

"We are not used to walking in these suits, only swimming in them," Diego snapped back.

The leader grunted and continued walking. Rreengrol pretended to help Fress up. Treela looked at them with questioning eyes, but Diego said nothing. They trudged toward blockish, windowless structures. Diego couldn't see any sign that anyone lived in the tallest building.

"In there," the leader said, his arm pointing to a narrow doorway in a smaller structure. "And then wait in the first room."

A Trolog led the way, and another one followed behind them. The room was large and empty.

Treela smiled and said, "You can take off your helmets in here. The air is even cleaner than nighttime outside."

"Indeed," Rreengrol replied. He glanced at Diego, who was already releasing the seals on his helmet. When he took it off, the air was better. It still had the antiseptic and recycled taste of a spaceship, but he would not complain. After the lake and the wind, this was better.

Another Trolog entered the room. When Fress and

Rreengrol removed their helmets, he gasped.

"What are you?" he growled.

"We are travelers from Amashi," Diego said. "We are accidental visitors."

"And they're also my friends," Treela added.

"Where are *you* from?" the leader asked, pointing to Diego. There was a slight pause for the translation.

"I am a citizen of the Seressin Empire and came here by accident. We arrived from Amashi."

"You look like us, but they…." The Trolog pointed to Fress and Rreengrol.

"…are also citizens of the Seressin Empire. We are part of a team exploring the ocean of Amashi. This is my friend, Rreengrol, and my other friend, Fress. I am Diego Perez."

The leader was speechless for a moment. Then his green eyes darkened. "You'll come with me. Someone higher than me can figure this out. Now!"

"Of course." Diego felt anything but calm, but he hoped he could keep his face passive.

A Trolog fell behind the foursome. Diego welcomed Treela's company, although he couldn't figure her out.

Me either.

Diego gazed at Fress but said nothing. Nor did he direct any thoughts to the Turengen. The group walked to the other end of the large room. A door slid open, and The Trolog leader motioned them in. The two Trologs stayed close but not close enough to touch them.

It was an elevator, but not as fast and smooth as those on the Seressin ships. The descent took forever, and near the end, the vibration made him nervous.

"Twenty floors below the surface," Treela announced. The guard leader glared at her.

Diego would have assumed at least twice that, but even

what she announced had him worried. If the elevators were in this kind of shape, he wondered what it was like this far beneath the planet's surface.

The door slid open, showing three other Trologs. They turned on their heels and walked down a well-lit corridor. Someone had painted decorations of various battles and conquests on the walls. Diego assumed it showed off Trolog power. It was faded and dusty and unimpressive to him.

The corridor curved to the right, with closed doors on either side. The company continued down the main corridor until the end, where two well-armored guards stood facing them. They had several side arms besides the large rifle-like weapons held in gauntleted hands. Diego heard a buzzing sound, and the guard stuck a small device in his ear. Diego believed it was a communicator.

"The Dominar will see the strangers now," the guard said, motioning them toward the door. It opened as he stepped away. The room before them had been decorated for a king with thick rugs woven in bright colors and golden highlights. Newer paintings on the walls showed space scenes and historical, land-based battles. Diego led the group in.

"Keep Captain Tremorin's daughter in the outer room," a voice bellowed.

Diego glanced at Treela, whose eyes glittered in anger. He didn't blame her for her irritation. The door slid shut in her face. Diego faced a man who resembled the leader of the group escorting them in. His almost white hair contained streaks of gray and black. He lounged in an overlarge chair. This Trolog wore a great deal of jewelry around his neck, wrists, and fingers. His uniform material was rich, and it fit a muscular frame. His green eyes were lighter than what Diego had seen so far.

Is this Trologar? Fress asked.

I don't know. Probably.

"Who are you, and why did you kidnap one of my people?"

"Dominar, I am Commander Diego Perez. This is my second in command, Rreengrol of Grrlock, and my Communications Officer, Fress, a member of the Turengen people. They are an essential part of my crew. Treela Tremorin came voluntarily with us, knowing we were going to bring her home."

"Commander, because of your station, I will have a room prepared for you while we consider your situation."

"And my crew?"

"First, I was addressing you, not your talking animals. We have a place to board animals."

Rreengrol stiffened beside Diego. Crackling sounded inside his mind. Fress was furious. "I find this conversation upsetting. I trust these two people, crewmates, who are very capable in their jobs. They are every bit as smart as you or me, probably smarter."

"A trained pranlis and a furry floritz."

"Dominar, I don't know what you have in mind for us, but we are citizens of the Seressin Empire. There should be diplomacy rather than insults. I think an apology is in order. While my crew is placed in unsuitable quarters, I refuse to stay in a decent room. We will stay together in the animal boarding place." Diego knew he was pushing his authority, but this pompous jackass had stomped on his last nerve.

Several Trologs gasped, and everything stopped for several seconds.

"You will not insult the Dominar!" The Trolog leader turned to the guard who had escorted them in. "Take them to the prisoner's quarters. Let them see how that suits them."

"Come with me." The guard grabbed Diego by the arm and jerked him forward.

Diego tossed his helmet to Rreengrol and grabbed for the guard with his free hand. In a move faster than the Trolog expected, Diego flipped him over his hip. Then he kneeled on the guard's chest with his arm against his neck. "I, too, do not wish to be insulted. We will accompany you. You do not need to use force."

No one spoke for several heartbeats. Diego got up and took the helmet back from Rreengrol. Diego reached his hand out to help the dazed guard up. The Trolog ignored it. As they left the room, the Dominar was silent.

Treela stood right outside the door. "What happened?"

"Go to your home," the guard growled, pushing her away.

"Be careful," Diego murmured to his guard. The soldier turned away. "We will be all right, Treela. A disagreement with your Dominar."

"What?" She stood gaping at them.

Diego and the others followed the corridor to another elevator. It rose back toward the surface. While it took longer, by the time it stopped, Diego figured they had to be close to the surface. The guards marched them out, then led them down another corridor. Grimy walls showed neglect, along with footprints in a layer of dust on the floor. Fewer lights shone, but Diego figured more sunlight got into this area.

Their Trolog escorts stopped and pushed a button next to a door. It slid open with a groan. "You have a weapon—a knife in the pocket of your suit. Give it to me!" Rreengrol complied. The guard motioned Rreengrol into the small cubicle.

"This cabin is larger than my first squire's cabin," he quipped. The door creaked shut behind him.

Fress was relieved of her small knife and motioned into the next cell.

A few more steps and Diego saw what he assumed was an identical holding cell. After being relieved of his weapon, they shoved him in, and the door slid shut. They left Diego in the darkness. He slipped on the helmet without sealing it and activated the lights. There was a threadbare pallet and a small hole in the ground in one corner. He could guess what that was for. He looked around and saw nothing else.

Diego pulled off the helmet and rubbed his eyes. A yawn followed. *Fress, you are going to have to be our communicator, but let's try to get some sleep first.*

Certainly, Commander.

Diego!

Yes, Diego.

He was even too tired to chuckle at the humorous tone of Fress's thoughts. Diego realized they were in a terrible situation, but he couldn't feel any accompanying emotions. He could only lay down and try to sleep.

CHAPTER THIRTY-ONE

The next morning, incredible heat woke Diego from a restless sleep. The morning sun shone through a small window at the back of the cell. When he looked, the huge red sun had just risen above the horizon. He couldn't imagine what it would be like later in the day. The wind kicked up, and dust particles danced and swirled throughout his cubicle. Sweat rolled down his face and inside his suit.

Fress?

Yes, Diego.

Are you two baking in the early morning sun?

Yes. They created these rooms for maximum discomfort.

Diego dragged his pallet to a place out of the sunlight, just under the window slot. It only helped a bit. He stripped off the Amashi environmental suit, trying to cool off in the soft one-piece undergarment. A jug stood near the door. It contained water, and Diego tried a sip. Not the most flavorful, and it already had a layer of dust. Still, it helped quench his thirst. He laid his suit across it to avoid more dust. There was wind, but not as strong as by the lake where they had been captured.

No one came by during the day—no meals, no more water. The environmental suit had run out of both items before their capture. The sun rose enough to quit shining through the window, but the heat was still oppressive. Diego wrote a few notes in the dust and played a couple of games by himself or mentally with Fress. He climbed up onto the windowsill, and while he could have squeezed out, the drop was too far. Their cells were at least three stories above the rocky ground.

He didn't see any guards, but Diego figured they didn't

need any. The sun would have given anyone outside a heat stroke, prisoners and guards alike. As the sun lowered in the west, Diego leaned over the sill to check the outer wall for any handholds. A few bricks and rocks jutted out, making escape difficult but not impossible. A door slammed below, and a lone guard came out of the building and started marching back and forth. After a while, he leaned against the building and dozed off. The guard would make it hard to escape.

Diego realized this was the tall building they had seen as they arrived in Trologar the previous night. And their cells were about halfway up. Not that it mattered.

Commander?

Yes.

Are we going to escape when the sun sets?

If the Trologs keep us in here, we must try. Would you be able to climb down?

Do not let my stubby fingers fool you. Turengens have claws.

There's a guard down there.

He's asleep.

Is Rreengrol good with this idea?

Rreengrol suggested it first.

Diego laughed. He perched himself on the windowsill, watching the shadows deepen on the east side of the building. The wind blew softer, still carrying thick dust, but despite that, it cooled his sweaty body.

Just as he was ready to test his wall-climbing skills, muffled footsteps sounded in the hall. They didn't stop until they reached his door. By then, he had pulled on the environmental suit.

The door opened, and a Trolog beckoned to him. Diego didn't move. "Do you always try to starve your prisoners?"

The guard made his motion more emphatic and barked an order. Knowing he had no leverage with this Trolog, Diego walked out of the cell. They didn't stop at the other cells.

Diego? Do you know what's going on?

No, Fress. I'm sure I'll be back, and then I'll update you.

Diego paid closer attention to his surroundings as they headed back down the elevator and then into the corridor leading to the Dominar's suite of rooms. Occasionally, a door opened, and he glimpsed inside. Men eating their meals. His stomach rumbled in response, and Diego realized he could have eaten that oversized centipede right now.

A door slammed shut as he passed by, but not before he spied a Trolog woman and several smaller Trologs. They were of a higher class, judging from the fancy embroidery and ribbons on both the woman and the children. Another guard fell in behind him as they approached the same room where he and the others had met the Dominar.

This time, he didn't have to wait. The doors slid open, and Diego walked to the Dominar's intricately carved seat with more confidence than he felt. He stood, waiting for the Trolog to begin the conversation, wondering how they were going to understand each other. His translator stopped working sometime since the last visit.

The Dominar put a small box on the table next to him. Then he began speaking. The box must have been the Trolog version of a translator. "Have you reconsidered?"

"Have I reconsidered what, Dominar?" Diego asked.

The Dominar frowned. "Taking my offer of more comfortable quarters."

"Does that include my crew?"

The Trolog leaned forward. "I am talking only to you."

"And I am speaking for my crew. They are intelligent beings, and if they can't be treated with the respect they deserve, I would rather stay with them." Diego considered everything going on. Then he had a quick flash of insight. "I suspect this is about more than a creature's skin covering, though, isn't it? This is about Amashi and what's there."

The Dominar jerked back and muttered something Diego couldn't hear.

Diego pushed the issue. He couldn't be any worse off. "What are you looking for on Amashi?"

"You found an entrance."

"The Portal?"

"Developed by our scientists," the Dominar snapped. "The technology is ours."

"Then you need to discuss this with the Seressin high commanders. I am only a sub-commander on a minor mission."

Again, the Dominar leaned forward. "What else did you find?"

Diego tried to keep his tone light. "A very nasty sea spider that tried to eat me and one of my crewmembers."

The Dominar didn't find this comment amusing. "What did you find in the wreckage?"

"Nothing. Coming through the portal was by chance."

The Dominar snorted. "Nothing at all? Not even the most insignificant artifact?"

"What are you looking for?"

The Trolog glared at him and said nothing else.

"Again, I think you'd be able to get farther discussing artifacts with the Seressin high command. I don't have that authority. However, I have the authority to demand fair treatment."

"I am being fair. Otherwise, I would have killed all of you for kidnapping one of our own."

Diego frowned. "I didn't kidnap Treela. And I can't negotiate for the Seressin Empire."

"Someone who is ambitious can always negotiate for what they want." The Trolog had a smug smile on his face.

"Someone who has honor will not negotiate for his own

benefit and comfort while his crew suffers. I will stay with my crew."

The room remained silent for a minute. Only the ticking of a large clock in one corner of the room broke the silence.

"Am I excused, sir?" Diego asked.

"I will treat your crew with the respect afforded to Trologs if you go back and find more artifacts. Our agreement, no governments or other negotiators."

Diego paused. Rreengrol and Fress were in worse shape than him. Another day in the dust and sun? He couldn't give in to the Trologs. He and the others would try to escape, steal a ship, and return to Amashi. Diego shook his head. "I can't sell my honor. Besides, the Seressin have better technology available to help you in your quest."

"Take him back to his cell," the Dominar growled.

CHAPTER THIRTY-TWO

The guard motioned, and Diego followed. This time, another guard fell in behind him.

Are you all right? came Fress's mental query after they had locked him back in his cell.

I'm all right. Another jug of water stood inside the door. *Did you two get any water?*

No.

Despite the lateness of the day, the heat was oppressive, so Diego pulled off his environmental suit, then sat on the windowsill and fumed. If they had wanted to show good faith, there would have at least been water for his companions. *We leave during the night. At least it will be cooler.*

Then something dropped on his head. Diego almost fell out of the window. He grabbed the sill.

Looking up, a thin rope dangled in front of his eyes. He tried to lean farther out to see who dropped it, but he couldn't tell. Diego caught it and pulled it inside the cell with him. *Fress! Can you tell who is above us?*

Yes, Treela.

And is the guard still out there?

Just outside the door.

Treela. Diego laughed. *Again, not surprising.* Now, to tie the rope onto something. Nothing. The pallet, the hole in the corner, the smooth flat door. He would have to thank her, anyway. Darkness settled in his room, and it grew much cooler. Diego slid on the environmental suit and then the helmet, wrinkling his nose at the fact he needed a shower.

He rolled up the rope and tied it around his waist, figuring they might need it later. Then he snatched up the jug, tying the end of the rope around the narrow neck and letting it dangle from his waist. Slipping through the window, Diego found bricks sticking out enough for his fingers to hold on to. It was a slow descent. Below, he found a brick sticking out far enough for one foot to stand on. *Fress, I'm finding enough handholds. Come on down.*

We are already climbing down.

Diego noticed the shadows on either side of him. His gloves helped him cling to the rocks, and Diego made his way down the side of the building, feeling for more hand and footholds. He didn't hear the guard, and it worried him.

Not awake!

Diego misjudged the ground, falling hard, and then worried that his awkward landing would wake the guard. Instead, he felt the tip of a knife against his neck. *Watch out!* He called.

Instead of an answer, Rreengrol and Fress leaped on the Trolog and wrenched the knife out of his hands. It wasn't the guard. This Trolog stood a little shorter and wore dark clothing of animal skins and sewn together pieces of cloth. He had a long beard and plaited dark hair down to his waist.

The sun had set before Diego climbed down the side of the building, but he still spied the unconscious guard stretched on the ground nearby. He untied the jug and handed it to Rreengrol. The Grrlock's eyes lit up, but he handed it to Fress for the first drink.

"Who are you?" Diego asked the newcomer.

The man shook his head, several well-plaited braids clacking together. Diego didn't have a working translator, and this other Trolog didn't either.

"He's an outland scavenger," a voice spoke up.

"Treela?"

"Yes. Why didn't you use the rope? It would have been so

much safer and faster."

"I had nothing to tie it to."

"Oh."

"But I appreciate the help. Isn't this going to get you in trouble?"

"I couldn't let you stay in there. It wasn't fair. The Dominar and Father were upset with me, anyway. After they captured you three, they confined me to my room. But they couldn't keep me there."

"Why is this outlander here?" Diego asked, bringing them back to the matter at hand. The Trolog gazed at each one of them.

"They come to check for prisoners. They help them escape if there are any here."

The bearded man spoke in whispers to Treela.

"He says he will take all of us to his home, where they will feed us and provide us a cool place to sleep." They talked some more.

"How safe is this place?" Rreengrol asked.

Treela shook her head. "As safe as any other place on Trolog. I haven't heard of my people making any raids because no one knows where the outlanders live. It's too tricky to send expeditions to find them."

Diego wondered why Treela's people didn't set ambushes for these outcasts. "And will these people answer some of our questions?"

"Yes, I believe they will. And if they can't, then I will try."

"What about your father?"

She sighed. "I love my father, but I didn't like what happened to you. I don't like how they sit down there and pretend everything's all right." She paused. "Commander, I didn't tell you everything about why we were on Amashi."

"I thought that might be the case, but we need to get out of here and then talk. The Dominar acted eager to negotiate with me. Or force me into some kind of alliance."

Treela spoke to the outland scavenger, and he motioned for them to follow him.

Wait. I need to get what we left behind, Fress said.

"Fress will be right back. She dropped something on the way in."

The Turengen pattered away, then returned in just a few minutes. She handed the heaviest pouch to Diego and another to Rreengrol. The outlander watched, only shifting from one foot to another.

As soon as Fress distributed the artifact bags, the group set off across the rocky wasteland. Amazingly, the Trolog kept to a steady trot in the near total darkness. Diego stumbled several times as he followed their guide. Rreengrol reached out to steady him. His friend didn't have the exceptional eyesight of cats on his world, but he could still see well in the dark.

As they continued, Diego wondered if they were just getting in deeper.

CHAPTER THIRTY-THREE

They walked the rest of the night. Occasionally, Diego heard a screech in the distance; other times, it sounded closer, but their Trolog guide didn't seem bothered by it. Something came close enough to rattle the rocks near them, and Diego wished for his pistol. The outlander made a coughing sound with a small barking noise at the end, and the creature backed away.

"Did you see that?" Diego asked Rreengrol.

"Yes, a small, furred animal standing about as high as my knee."

"Shorter than a Turengen," Fress added.

"Am I the only one with poor night vision?" Diego muttered.

"I guess," Rreengrol said with a snicker. "But you have other talents."

Diego snorted, but Rreengrol didn't elaborate on any of those talents.

By the time they reached the base of the mountains he had seen in the distance from his cell window, Diego could barely put one foot in front of the other. Diego figured they had distanced themselves enough from Trologar to avoid detection, so he took a quick look with his light on its dimmest setting. When he saw the steep ascent, he wished he hadn't.

The outlander began talking to Treela. Then she turned to Diego. "We are following a path into their, uh, I don't know the Seressin word for it. I think it's 'house.' He asks you not to use your light. If you are worried about falling, then we can use the rope to tie us together." She pantomimed, but her Seressin had been clear. Rrishan was an excellent teacher.

"If it gets too steep, then we will."

She didn't answer but continued trudging behind the outlander.

Diego wondered at the Trolog outlander's ability to walk this rock-strewn route in the dark without the slightest hesitation. Perhaps the Dominar had so many prisoners these Trologs made frequent treks to the underground city to get them.

"Yes, he has walked this path often," Fress acknowledged.

The Trolog stopped and pointed toward a hidden crevasse. A dry, scraggly bush grew next to it. Treela ducked and pushed her way inside. The Trolog motioned for them to join her. Diego felt his way inside, some of the dry twigs snapping against his body, and found a very comfortable cavern inside. In the dim light, he noticed pallets, jugs, what looked to be bowls, and various other things unfamiliar to Diego. In the back of the cave, he heard a small rivulet of water splashing into a bowl-like depression. They finished the water in the jug during their trek, so this beckoned. Fress chittered her approval.

"Our guide says this is the place where we rest and prepare for the remainder of the journey when the sun sets," Treela explained.

"Tell him thank you. We are most grateful."

Treela did, and he grinned and then gave a small bow. He spoke again.

"He says he is curious to know about you and your friends but will wait until we reach his people."

Diego thought it might take a long time with only Treela translating. "Hopefully, you won't get too tired translating for all of us."

She shook her head. "I don't think so. This is rather exciting, almost as exciting as being in Father's spaceship."

"This outlander doesn't seem too different from the people in your city, other than the way he's dressed." Diego wasn't sure how to ask about his bedraggled appearance.

Treela glanced down at her Amashi suit. "I have heard rumors the scavengers dress that way to make our people think they are barely making it in the wilderness."

"It must work."

"Yes," Treela replied. "He says we can refresh, eat whatever food is here, and then rest and sleep." Their Trolog guide drank some of the water and grabbed something out of a container. He sat just inside the entrance. The reddish light from outside told them the sun had risen.

"No one has ever caught a scavenger or found out where they go?" Rreengrol asked.

"No, but then, the Dominar has only been obsessed by Amashi."

"Considering you have the technology for space travel, I can't see why your people wouldn't be able to locate escaped prisoners and outlanders," Diego mused.

"We only have a few old spaceships. My father's ship is the only one able to fly right now. The Dominar wishes to find the...the weapons that were invented on Amashi, or Treleesh, as our ancients called it."

Diego figured it had to be something like that. "To destroy the outlanders?"

"And the people of the nearest star system. The Dominar desires to be the ruler of an empire. I guess like you are part of."

"It took the Seressin millennia to build what they have," Diego protested. "I don't approve of all of their history and tactics, but I haven't read of them destroying inhabitants of star systems."

Treela sighed. "The more I learn, the more angry I am at our leadership."

If what the Amashina told Diego was true, did anyone need such a weapon? Even the Seressin? That thought disturbed him. "I agree with you. Is that what you didn't tell me before?"

"Yes," Treela said. "I was so proud when Father said I could go along with him on his ship. We would be explorers like our ancestors. We would find new worlds. And when the time came, I would follow him."

Diego nodded. "What changed your mind?"

"You and your crew. Rrishan and the others. I saw someone who looked like us working with others who didn't. And you didn't mind."

"Perhaps in my old life, I wouldn't have been so open-minded."

"Tell me about your old life."

"After we get something to drink and see what's here to eat," Diego said with a chuckle. They joined Rreengrol and Fress at the little pool of water. Diego held his hands under the small waterfall and then took a long drink. The water tasted fresher than any he'd had in a long time. Rreengrol checked the various containers. They contained tiny breads like crackers and dried strips with mixed flavors—meat and vegetables. Like the water, it tasted good.

Soon, they all lounged on pallets near the wall. Even though the air felt cooler inside the cave than their cells had been, the heat of the day found its way inside. Diego and the others pulled off their environmental suits. "How did you keep your suit?" he asked Treela.

"I took it off when I got home. Told my parents I had sent it down to the science lab and told the scientists I would send it down the next day after Father had time to look more closely at it. When I decided to help you escape, I just put it back on and slipped out."

Rreengrol laughed and stood up. He stretched his tail and then flicked it from side to side. "Sorry, but it had gone to sleep after being kinked up in my suit for so long."

Treela stared at his tail as though it were a separate entity. "What do you use it for?"

Rreengrol's yellow eyes widened. "What do I use it for?" He looked over his shoulder at his waving appendage. "Uh, it's part of me. It helps me with balance. Especially when I'm fighting."

"Oh. Sorry, I'd been wondering and never asked Rrishan about hers. I understand why you would want to move it around."

"I'm not offended."

She looked a bit confused.

"It doesn't bother me you're staring at my tail," Rreengrol explained.

"You were going to tell me about your old life. Before you became a commander." Her cheeks flushed pink as she turned back to Diego. "I can't believe you and I are about the same age, and you are already commanding a ship."

"To be honest, I can't either."

"Tell me where you came from?"

"Earth. I was the younger son of a rich landowner. We had many horses and cattle. He hired many vaqueros to care for the cattle and servants to take care of the casa grande." Diego had to explain some of his words and drew pictures in the dust of cattle and horses. He didn't do them justice. He told her about Tejas, the gelding he had trained and ridden across the hills of the rancho. And he remembered Fuerte, the reop he had befriended. He didn't compare to the gracefulness of a beautiful horse, but riding him was like riding through the clouds.

"How did you end up with the Seressin Empire?"

Diego yawned. "How about I explain after we sleep?" He felt Fress dozing against his side.

"Yes, you are right." Treela smiled. "Thank you for letting me see how beautiful your world is."

"Not everything was beautiful, but then no place is all

ugly."

"Trolog is."

"You said there were pleasant parts."

"I changed my mind. Let me know when you find something nice," she said as she settled down on her pallet.

"I will." Diego let the Turengen lie on the pallet they had shared, and he found another one near the opposite wall. Diego felt the hard stone under the pallet, but his exhaustion caused him to fall asleep within a few minutes.

———

The air pressed down on him, heavy like before a powerful storm. No, this was worse than a storm. He stood near a grove of trees. Their leaves drooped. Long, thin branches reached for the ground rather than up toward the sun. Golden clouds veiled the sun, a large, deep red orb. The turquoise sky was so deep that Diego felt he could stretch out and dip his fingers in it.

When he reached, though, a flying insect with wings as transparent as spider silk landed on his finger. It had a body as thin as a pen. Its color was also turquoise-colored, blending with the sky so the wings didn't seem attached to anything. The creature's feet tickled, and Diego smiled at this beautiful thing. He glanced at the sun, wondering where he had seen one like it before. Not on his home world. Nor on Koress. No matter.

He gazed at his feet, which were covered in light green moss. Diego spied a line of fuzzy-looking ants making their way to a distant mound. A little farther away flowed a small stream where two long, eel-like fish leaped from the water and into the air, their fins flapping as though they could fly. Then, they both turned back to the water and were soon gone.

With so many curious and beautiful things, Diego wondered why he felt so oppressed. The air closed in on him, as well as the ground. He heard a rumble from far away. The ground rippled toward him. It coursed under his feet, knocking him to the ground. He remembered earthquakes, but this was more. Diego jerked his eyes toward a distant horizon and spied a large blossoming cloud shaped like a tree, the trunk growing, growing, and growing into the blue sky. First, it glowed so bright it hurt his eyes, then it darkened until it turned black. The turquoise sky also darkened until it became an angry, reddish-brown radiating out like the spokes on a wagon wheel.

The wind came next, racing across the ground toward him like stampeding cattle, gathering soil, rocks, and vegetation. He felt terror when he saw the wind but couldn't do a thing. He couldn't move, couldn't run. The wall came toward him. It engulfed him, picked him up, and carried him into the air. He felt his skin peeling away, and then he became a skeleton blowing apart in the horrible hot wind....

CHAPTER THIRTY-FOUR

"Commander," Fress called. She had a hand on his arm, gently squeezing it until he awakened. "You were dreaming."

"Dreaming? Again?" Diego rubbed his hand down his pants. His legs were still there. His hands and arms were still there.

"Yes," she hissed.

Diego recalled his dream and realized it had been a short one. A few streaks of sunlight still shone on the ceiling. The others were still asleep, so he hadn't shouted out loud. The Trolog dozed against the rocky entrance of the cave.

Fress sat beside him. "Our guide is very sure of our safety."

This dream was every bit as bad as the one he had during the visit to Koress when he was a new squire. Diego glanced at his hands and saw them shake. He knew this dream was worse; he couldn't change anything he had seen. It happened in the past. How did he know this? He just did. "Did you see it? My dream?"

Fress shook her head. "Only felt something terrible. Saw tiny flashes of the dream. Something powerful. Something that could kill many beings. What do you think it is?"

"My dream showed something happening long ago. It reminded me of what the Amashina told us about the colossal explosion in their past."

"Were you seeing what happened there?"

"No. I think this occurred someplace else." Diego still felt foggy from sleep. Where had he seen such a sun? Then he almost smacked himself. Trolog! "My dream was something happening here! In the past. They were doing the same thing here as they did on Amashina. But why?"

"And how could someone forget such a terrible thing?" Fress asked.

"This is something else to talk about when we get to the Trolog sanctuary." Diego went over to the pool of water and drank his fill. Then he washed his face and as much of his body as his sense of propriety allowed him. He pulled out one of the dried meat and fruit strips, snapped it in half, and sat with Fress, savoring the flavors of the food.

Fress dozed against his side as she had when they had first arrived. He didn't mind. After his dream, though, Diego felt restless. He pulled away from the Turengen so she could continue sleeping. Quietly, he stepped toward the entrance and stopped next to the outlander guide, still within the cave's entrance.

The sun shone like a monstrous red platter with fiery edges. He tried to study it between his fingers. Blinking, he backed away and noticed the Trolog gazing at him. Diego didn't explain what he was doing, not quite understanding it himself. He stepped back into the coolness of the cave, then lay down and fell into a dreamless sleep.

When he woke up, the Trolog made a few hand motions, telling him they needed to go. Diego awakened Rreengrol, Treela, and then Fress. A pinkish cast colored the sky when they set out on the narrow path leading farther up in the mountains. By the time it grew dark, they had crested one of the steep foothills and headed into a valley.

Diego heard the rustling of various creatures. He trusted their guide to know which sounds belonged to friendly beings and which didn't. When they reached the bottom of the mountain pass, they walked along a narrow path. Diego wished he could shine a light to see what they were passing through. It sounded like water nearby and it continued to follow them, so he figured they walked beside a stream or river. He wondered how much vegetation grew in these mountains.

Diego quit speculating and concentrated on his steps in the darkness. It seemed to be easier this night, but he didn't want to make any mistakes and fall on his face. The first moon rose, giving them a little light. The path crossed to the other side of the valley, near a stream flowing out from a mountain crevice.

They began walking uphill. This time, the trail was steeper. He kept his eye on Treela. They crested the mountain, and Diego saw more stars in the sky above him. They reassured him.

They were heading down the slope when Treela stopped. Diego took a couple of steps, almost plowing into her. He heard a low conversation in front of them, and then they continued. Other outlanders had joined their group. He could see a vague shape sitting on a boulder next to the path and figured it was an outlander sentry.

They reached another cave entrance, but the outlander waited a few moments before entering. This cavity didn't have a pool of water, only a narrow crevice going inside the mountain. The path sloped downward, and after making a curve, Diego noticed artificial lighting along the way—dim at first, then brighter. The air felt cool, with an earthy scent much more refreshing than what he had experienced on the surface. They walked for quite a distance until they reached a huge cavern. It would have been large enough to have accommodated everyone in the pueblo back on his home planet, Diego thought. Other Trologs waited there, motioning for them to sit on the floor. Diego and his companions sat and waited. Many outlanders sat with them, wearing new-looking clothing—tunics and trousers of finely woven cloth.

Diego wondered about this cavern. The ceiling rose so high that he couldn't see all of it, but he spied various colored stalactites over his head. They were more impressive than the most elaborate church he had been in.

Several Trologs brought out trays of food, much of which

he didn't recognize, but it all looked fresh and smelled good. A few older Trolog outlanders came and joined them. They motioned for everyone to eat. Diego reached for a tuber-like food, broke it apart, and took a nibble. It crunched into smaller pieces and had a sweet flavor, somewhat like sugar cane imported from the Indies. More food came around on different-colored platters. He tried several more before he just leaned back and rested. A dust-free cool breeze drifted through the cavern. Everyone seemed friendly, and he was off his feet.

"Did you find the food to your taste?"

Diego jerked in surprise. He expected Treela would have to translate for everyone. He hadn't thought the outlanders would have translators. The Trolog who approached him was thinner and shorter than the Dominar. He smiled, took Diego's plate, and handed it to a boy. This Trolog's raven-black hair contained white streaks, telling the young sub-commander this was an older man. Diego wondered what they thought of his almost black hair. "It is all very good, sir." A pendant hung around the Trolog's neck and Diego guessed this was the translation device.

A group of seven other Trologs stood behind him. "Our ability to comprehend your language surprises you?"

"Yes, sir," Diego replied. "We had translators, but we left them behind on Amashi, or I believe you call it Treleesh."

The older man nodded, holding up his pendant. "There has been no use for them until now, so we only have a few of them."

Diego introduced himself and his companions.

"I am Storeem, the leader of this society. And these are members of our leadership group. Rinstrom, in charge of our community's environment, Torin, in charge of food and supplies, Huliss, our head scientist." Storeem introduced Diego to four others who had charge of medical, manufacturing, emergencies, and diplomacy.

"Diplomacy?" Diego began. "Are you in contact with the Dominar?"

Clorin, the head of diplomacy, grimaced. "No, Commander, we are not, other than to relieve him of his prisoners. We are not the only mountain community. There are several, and we have diplomats to make sure our relations remain open and cordial."

"Seems smart to me."

"Please do not be insulted, Commander," Storeem said. "But despite your dark hair, you seem rather young to be in charge of a mission to a planet."

"Though young, my task was supposed to be routine, to monitor an outlying planet avoided by Seressin commanders. My commander, Marix Ziron, trusted me to give greetings to the Amashina leadership and then take a bit of leave with my crew. Trolog would be a planet more to my commander's liking."

Storeem smiled. "Perhaps and perhaps not."

Diego's dream nagged at him. "May I ask a question without insult?"

"Of course."

"When we first landed on Amashi, we were told of an incident many generations ago where some of your ancestors landed on the largest land mass, built a community, and then blew themselves up with a weapon of horrifying power. Did the same thing happen on Trolog?"

Treela's breath hissed between her teeth. "The forbidden; the forgotten history...."

CHAPTER THIRTY-FIVE

Even the outlander Trologs jerked back in surprise, and Diego wondered what hornet's nest he might have stirred up.

"Yes," Storeem said. "Some would like to forget, but you only need to go out during the day, see the scoured land and wasted atmosphere to remember."

"How did you find out?" Treela snapped.

Diego drew in a deep breath. "I saw it in a dream. It was more real than when the Amashina described it on their planet. I felt like I was there."

Treela paused in thought. "A dream? You put stock in dreams?"

"Most of the time, I don't even remember my dreams, but there have been some in the past year and a half that either foretold events or recounted them. I could change some happenings in the former, but this one terrified me. I have seen nothing like it. In my dream, this weapon stripped the skin from my body." He gazed at Storeem. "Is that what this weapon did?"

"Yes, according to the records we found. It killed most of the population of our planet. The way you described and then later, when we had no food, clean water, or shelter against the sun and the wind."

"What was this weapon's purpose?" Diego turned to Treela. "You said the Dominar wanted a weapon to make him the ruler of an empire. This weapon? How would he decide who deserved to die or not?"

"I don't know. I didn't know what my father went to Amashi for, but it seems he was looking for one of these weapons."

"Such a weapon should never be used against an inhabited

world," Diego stated.

The rest of the group sat listening in horrified attention. Finally, Rreengrol spoke up. "Would such a thing still be working if it's been sitting in the ocean all this time?"

"Probably not," Storeem said. "But even unexploded, it could be dangerous because the fuel for such a weapon is poisonous."

"Your father looked for evidence of such a device," Diego suggested to Treela. "The device that exploded and destroyed the only decent-sized landmass on Amashi. It destroyed all the Trologs living there. Would there have been another? One that didn't explode? Or was he looking for the instructions on how to build one of these?"

Storeem leaned forward. "The record says the information was being sent back and forth. How, we don't know, but both groups worked on these weapons. It said there might have been two such weapons on the planet you called Amashi."

"We need to get back and tell the Amashina."

"And if you find the other weapon or the information on how to make one?" Storeem asked.

"I don't know," Diego murmured. "I am not a full commander, but such a weapon is too dangerous for anyone to possess."

"It is enough right now that you understand the horror of such a thing."

"Hopefully, the ocean has destroyed it as well."

"Hopefully."

Rinstrom broke the long pause. "We have rooms where you can rest. Tomorrow, we will show you around our underground city."

"Thank you." Diego spoke for all his crew. He could talk with Storeem tomorrow about how to get back to Amashi. Maybe these people had ships since they seemed farther advanced than the people in Trologar.

Still, Treela's father had the route. Getting that might be trickier than getting a ship. Diego lay awake in a comfortable cave room with his crew, listening to the sounds of them sleeping. He pondered Storeem's question—what if he found such a device? Duty said he should turn it over to Marix Ziron, but could he? Knowing what it did? With a sigh, he rolled over, hoping he wouldn't find this device or have to make that decision.

CHAPTER THIRTY-SIX

What the outlanders had built underground was impressive. Although Diego had seen little of Trologar, this seemed much cleaner. It looked more—he fumbled for the word—industrious. Men and women strode the halls with purpose. Storeem took them to a place where merchants sold their wares. Diego saw clothing of all kinds, crafted items, and even food shops.

"I wonder where they grow their food," Rreengrol murmured.

Storeem must have heard him because the underground farms were next on the tour. They devoted one whole cavern to growing ground plants and small trees. The lights felt like the sun on his home world. Diego's estimation of these people grew. The outlanders dedicated a separate cavern to the growth of animals, most of them like the centipedes.

"Why are you allowing me to see this?" Treela asked when they had gone down to the lower levels. "How do you know I am not going back home?"

"You came with these people. You were helping them escape. Were you not going to continue to help them after their escape?" Storeem asked in his gentle voice.

"I may want to go home someday."

"That would not surprise me. And someday we would like to negotiate with Trologar. It would be good to have someone who could speak for us."

"Me?"

"Why not?"

Treela's argument seemed to have dissolved. "You trust me?"

"Of course, Treela Tremorin."

"You know who I am?"

"Yes, you are the daughter of Trologar's number one explorer and the Dominar's right-hand man."

"How did you know?"

"We have rebuilt some communications devices the ancients had. Those have made it possible to hear communications with your spaceship and in Trologar, too. Besides, it was easily guessed from our conversations."

"Oh."

"Do you have starships?" Diego asked.

"No," Storeem said. "We have the hulls and parts of old spacefaring vessels, but we do not have any working spacecraft."

"How are we going to return to Amashi?"

"You came through a portal from Amashi, correct?"

"Yes, and we tried to go back into the lake and find it, but we had no luck."

Storeem looked thoughtful. "How did it open on the other end? We only have small bits of information about this thing the ancients called a black hole portal; just enough to know it existed."

"This one activated when someone got close to the entrance."

"And it didn't happen on Trolog when you tried to go back."

"No. We swam most of the lake's depths and are pretty sure we were in the same place we came out."

"Then it must not work in both directions."

"No," Diego affirmed. "We had to leave the lake because the suit's air systems couldn't handle the pollution."

Storeem bowed his head as though meditating. "Then there is only the Dominar's ship."

Diego frowned. "I have never stolen a ship before."

Rreengrol cleared his throat.

"Well, not a ship of that size."

"What difference does it make?" Rreengrol asked. "One has to make a plan and get the right people to make it work."

"Are you serious?" Treela demanded. "You'd try to steal my father's ship?"

"We must go back. If there is an unexploded device, we must find and then deactivate it."

"And then give it to the Seressin, your masters?" Treela snapped.

Before Diego could make any kind of answer, Fress said, "Do you think the Dominar deserves it?"

Treela sighed. "No, I believe no one deserves it."

"Treela, I agree with you," Diego insisted.

She gazed at him, her green eyes penetrating. "Do you mean that?"

"Yes."

"But you are a sworn commander of the Seressin Empire," Rreengrol reminded him.

"I am, and I don't know what's going to happen, but we have to warn the Amashina of what might threaten their world."

Storeem gazed at each speaker. "I will gather our best outland agents, and we will make a plan to get you back to Amashi."

Diego couldn't help but wonder at Storeem's willingness to help them. "Thank you."

"I don't think we need to wait long before we do this," Storeem continued. "Do you think three of you can pilot such a ship?"

"Four," Treela declared.

"Four," the Trolog leader corrected. "But you will go against the will of your father and the Dominar."

Treela looked thoughtful. "I wish I could do this without

hurting my father, but I don't like the Dominar. What might happen if he has one of the ancients' weapons?"

Diego nodded. He couldn't agree more. He turned his attention back to Storeem. "Back to the question of piloting the ship. Some jobs can be learned quickly if there are some of your people willing to come. Besides, I have not piloted this ship either, so I need to learn, too. Especially considering this ship can go underwater. That's quite an accomplishment."

Treela looked smug.

"Such technology belonged to the ancients, discovered just before the destructive bombs," Storeem pointed out. "But your father figured it out and took the ship into space again. That's the real accomplishment. We have scientists who could fill positions on your father's ship. In fact, we rescued several who have knowledge of piloting a spaceship. They made the mistake of speaking against the Dominar."

"I think we should scout the place where they keep the ship," commented Rreengrol.

"I think so, too. We need to know how well it's guarded and the best way to capture it," Diego added. "And I agree it needs to be soon. Do you know where the space field is?"

"I do," Treela said. "But only from Trologar."

"We know the way," Storeem assured her. "I will speak with the scientists and find out which of them will go on a space mission. It is late today. We will meet early tomorrow and make plans."

Diego wondered how someone could be so calm when so much depended on their success.

CHAPTER THIRTY-SEVEN

Two days later, three Trologs and the three Seressin warriors trekked along primitive mountain paths toward the old Trolog spaceport. They left the outlander city just before the huge red sun finished slipping beyond the horizon behind them. It would take all night to reach the site. Diego thought it ironic that it lay closer to the outlanders than Trologar. This time he and the others wore night lenses, as well as attire more suitable to this environment.

Diego hoped the Dominar's guards around the spaceship were just as complacent as the ones at the old city.

Only a few animals approached them. The first mammalian animal he saw on this planet fascinated Diego. It appeared to be between the size of a rat and a cat. The creature had, as best as he could see with the lenses, a short, bristly pelt. Ears stood high, almost as large as the animal's head, and they swiveled forward and back. The eyes were large and luminous, and its nose pointed. It scuttled on top of a boulder and stared at them from a short distance away, then leaped into the deep shadows.

"A shedu. They mostly eat insects. Related to a pranlis."

"This shedu looked like a mammal." When Tendar, the leader of the group, said nothing, Diego added, "Warm-blooded, like us."

"There are not as many warm-blooded animals as there are hard-skinned creatures. And most are nocturnal, as, I suppose, we are."

They continued walking in relative silence. Another animal approached them, resembling the centipede they had killed at the lake. It howled its displeasure when their guide leaped forward and touched one leg with the end of his stick.

"Obviously, not a plain walking stick," Diego commented through his translator.

"No, it's a stun stick. The only trick is shocking it before it can sneak up and attack. Most of the higher life forms are already aware of these weapons and stay away."

"How handy," Rreengrol added. "We must negotiate for some of those. And these night lenses, which are superior to ours."

"One thing at a time," Tendar said with a soft laugh.

"Yes, we have to make it back first." Diego glanced up and noticed a few stars trying to glitter through the haze. He compared them to the Trolog people. They were like the few stars trying to get beyond their horrific past. Storeem's people seemed to do it with dignity. The Dominar's people? Diego steered away his judgments. He hadn't been here long enough to judge them. And Treela? Diego had a hard time figuring her out. He liked her and wanted to know her better. And then she'd do or say something snide or accusing, and he felt frustrated, only wishing to strangle her. Her loyalties seemed to waffle, too.

A creature fluttered overhead. Was it a bird or maybe a bat? The creature's long, waving wings were almost white on a mouse-sized body. It, too, had over-sized ears, and it landed on a stunted tree with something struggling in its clawed feet. Snapping down on its prey, it leaped up and flew away with the limp body. Tendar didn't venture to tell him about this creature, and Diego didn't ask. He could ask Storeem when they were back in the outlander's city. "Tendar, what do you call your city?"

"It is simply the First Refuge."

"Makes sense."

Commander.

Yes, Fress?

May I intrude?

You have already.

She coughed and didn't continue.

I'm just teasing, Fress. I suppose I am broadcasting my thoughts all over the place.

Yes. You are worried with reason. These are a complicated species. Understanding them is difficult.

I'm sorry if I am putting you in an uncomfortable position.

That is all right. We are just another 'weapon' in the arsenal.

The comparison startled Diego, who chose not to follow up on Fress's assessment. They could talk about it later. *Is there something I should know about Treela?* He watched Tendar's back, all the while paying attention to Fress.

Her loyalty — no. Treela admires the outlanders, as well as sympathizing with them. She is afraid of the Dominar. She also fears for her father, and she likes you.

Me?

Yes. Fress stopped communicating.

Diego sensed there was more, but the Turengen hesitated to tell him. *Just let me know if anyone becomes a danger to our mission.*

I will.

They continued through the night, stopping occasionally to get a drink and take a quick rest while they ate a snack. Diego's anxiety increased, and he tried to tamp it down. He had no reason to worry right now. He wished someday the commanders would send him on a mission that was actually simple. Then he sighed. Since the Seressin captured him, he had fought to become a free citizen. Maybe this was what being free meant — making hard decisions.

The hills ahead of them glowed in the early morning sunrise when they reached the valley where the spaceship rested. While four of them found vantage points in the rocks and began watching the activities in the area below, the others put together several camouflaged tents to protect them from the rays of the red sun.

CHAPTER THIRTY-EIGHT

Diego exchanged his night vision goggles for shaded day goggles. As the sun came up, the activity below slowed and then ended. Everyone who had been working when the reconnaissance group arrived now sheltered in the ship or in the buildings. Diego continued to watch until the heat became unbearable and the light too bright, even for the darkened goggles. No one worked outside, and no one moved from one place to another. "Let's get under cover."

Fress was the first one in the shelter. She looked like a wet rug.

Rreengrol appeared little better. "Didn't think you'd ever come in out of the sun."

Treela said nothing.

They grabbed breakfast and a full container of water and relaxed. Tendar joined them.

"What are your thoughts, Diego?" Rreengrol asked.

"The best success is raiding at night," Diego began. "That's not the case here. The best time to capture the spacecraft is during the day."

"But that's the worst time to be outside!" Treela declared.

"We'll have to figure out how to protect ourselves," Diego replied. "Use the shelter material or something similar. Treela, do you know if there are devices that can detect movement at a distance?"

"Probably not. No one figures there'd be anyone crazy enough to be out during the day."

"I've been called crazy before."

"But it is a real danger," Tendar added. "To be out for too

long."

"If we plan well and execute quickly, we won't be out that long," Diego pointed out.

"We will watch and record everything for the next few nights."

"Two nights, and then we present a plan to Storeem. We can't let this go too long," Diego insisted.

They took turns sleeping, and Diego occasionally stole out to see if anything was going on. Activity resumed before the red sun reached the western horizon. Heavy boxes were on mechanized carts, but the procession looked like a line of ants heading to the spaceship's cargo hold.

Rreengrol slipped up beside him. "Anything?"

"I think so. It appears the ship is being restocked."

Rreengrol studied the scene below and then nodded. "I think you're right, but when are they going to take off?"

"We need to find out. I don't want to go back to the First Refuge and the ship take off while we're gone." Diego noticed the Trologs had protective gear, including helmets. If he got one, no one would notice his dark hair. "I'm going down. I should be back before too long."

"Wait a minute!" Rreengrol protested. "You need a partner."

"Rreengrol, you'd stick out like a wolf in a sheep pen, and they might recognize Treela. I'm the only one who could get away with eavesdropping."

Rreengrol growled. "I hate it when you're right. Be careful."

Diego smiled. "When Fress wakes up, tell her what happened and have her keep tabs on me."

"Sure thing, Commander."

Diego kept as much to the shadows as he could, although that was difficult in the bright sunlight. By the time he reached the valley floor, the red sun was behind the mountains, and shadows had deepened. He stalked between stacks of crates and canisters. A Trolog worker came his way, and Diego slipped behind a stack of supplies, waiting. The man came closer, and Diego could tell the worker was about his size. A little closer, then he pounced, taking the Trolog to the ground.

Diego was lucky. The ambush knocked the worker unconscious.

He pulled off the lightweight work suit and the helmet and realized that he was a she. Diego dragged her behind a stack of supplies, found some rope-like material, and tied her up. He would have an outlander carry her back up to their camp. The work suit was tight across his shoulders, but it would do.

Diego grabbed her cart and noticed that when he rolled it next to a stack of boxes, they stuck to it. He didn't try pulling them off. Diego watched the roadway ahead of him. Luckily, a gentle light bathed the ship, including the open hatch.

I am awake now, Commander.

Fress, could you send an outlander down to the valley to pick up the worker I ambushed? She doesn't need to tell anyone there's a spy on the loose.

Yes, sir.

Diego kept his translator on. He left his cart and snuck around other bundles, piles, and mounds of supplies, trying to get as close to other Trologs as he could.

"Why so soon?" came a clear voice. The person answering was more soft-voiced, and Diego couldn't understand the answer. Frustrated, he moved closer to a Trolog who appeared to be in a leadership position.

"Crew supplies? Food and water?" the clear-voiced Trolog asked.

"Yes, sir. Ample. We can replenish any shortages at the destination spaceport."

"Good. We need to have all the weaponry checked out."

"Yes, sir."

But when is the launch? Diego fumed.

"Seems rather short notice and the height of impatience," still another voice muttered not too far away.

Diego tried to embrace the shadows, willing everyone not to see him.

"Even for the Dominar."

"Careful, Supervisor."

"I know, but sending the ship up so soon without full maintenance...day after tomorrow."

"We don't have to go up in it," the first Trolog said with a chuckle.

"True. And the scientists are doing their work during the sleep cycles."

Two nights! There was no time to work out a strategy with the outlanders. They would have to use the people they had and take the ship. Diego slipped back through the shadows toward the foot of the mountain and met the outlander carrying a squirming Trolog over his shoulder. They trekked up the path as quickly as possible.

Tendar said something Diego couldn't hear, and the captive grew quiet. Tendar and Diego were panting by the time they reached the secret camp. The Trolog took his prisoner inside the shelter while Diego waited outside.

"What did you find out?" Rreengrol asked. "You weren't down there long."

"Found out what I needed to know," he said, puffing, his hands on his knees. "And we won't have time to plan much of anything. They're taking the ship up in two days."

CHAPTER THIRTY-NINE

Rreengrol stared at him. "What? But the scientists...."

Diego drew in a deep breath. "Tellis has much stamina. He and I can get back to the city and bring whatever scientists are willing to come. We should be back here in time."

Rreengrol's golden eyes widened. "He's willing to do that? Do you think you can keep up with him?"

Diego frowned. "The night vision lenses help. I can do it."

Rreengrol nodded.

"Let me catch my breath, and then we'll go," Diego said. He gathered a water container, pulled off the work suit and helmet, and then took a quick drink.

Soon, he and Tellis, a small, wiry Trolog, were trotting along the path back toward the city. This time, while Diego heard various creatures, he didn't pay attention to them. His only goal was to keep up with the outlander and later return to the spaceship. Tellis stopped twice during the night, and just about the time Diego figured he had caught his breath, the outlander took off down the trail. He was a Trolog of few words, too.

When they reached the hidden entrance to the outlander city, the sky was only beginning to grow pink in the East. Storeem waited in the cavern.

"How did you know?" Diego wheezed.

"Come, we'll walk down to the meeting hall, and I'll explain. After the meeting, you can rest."

"How did you know?" Diego repeated when they arrived at the meeting place.

"Tellis has a communicator and sent us a coded message."

"Then I didn't need to come back." Irritation flickered, but

Diego waited for the explanation.

"You needed to come, Commander. You need to meet those who will be part of your crew. Some of these people have worked on the ship before. They are invaluable, and they needed to meet the person who would be commanding them so they could get to know him. Especially since that captain is so young."

"Do you think that will be a problem?"

"I hope not, especially after you have talked to them, and they know your experience."

That made sense, and Diego offered no more protests. Instead, after a quick meal, he sat down with a dozen men and women of various ages and discussed the upcoming voyage. Storeem brought in another dozen outlanders.

"These will help you take the ship. You will work out a strategy when you are back at the surveillance site."

"Yes, I have been thinking about that." Diego offered his idea of taking the ship during the day. Several of the Trologs gazed at him as though he were demented, but the soldier outlanders understood the wisdom of that move. "I would prefer to take the ship with a minimum of casualties," Diego concluded.

"It will have to be a quick raid," a burly Trolog pointed out. "We have neither the stamina to fight in the heat of the day nor do we want to give the Dominar's people time to mount a defense or destroy the ship."

"They have been working until shortly after the sun rises. Some go in the ship, and the rest go into a building on the other side of the valley," Diego explained. "They would be more fatigued by then, sleepy and less attentive. My idea is to go in right after sunrise, bar the entrance of the living quarters, and then take the ship."

"And if the ship is locked?"

"There should be more than one hatch. Treela Tremorin could give the location of other hatches. Especially if there is an emergency hatch."

"Are you sure of her loyalty?"

"I have the means to know if anyone's loyalty changes," Diego stated without mentioning Fress. Let them guess, he thought.

Several asked about his background, which he discussed with them. "I am not afraid to ask for advice if I need it. Many of you are much more adept at the science of this ship. That's how I have been able to advance — that and some luck."

"What happens when we take our ship back to the water planet and these Seressin are there? What will they do with us — or to us?"

"I will report to my marix and make recommendations."

"And this marix will listen to you and follow those recommendations?"

Diego thought about Marix Ziron and his sometimes-quick temper. "I think he will listen to me. As to making you some kind of prisoner, I doubt it. They might want to recruit your system into the empire, but that part's your decision."

"What about the weapon?" That was Storeem.

Diego sighed. "If I am asked about it, I will have to report that information to my superiors. However," Diego paused, then answered honestly. "I hope there isn't any weapon or at least one that works, and then I hope I make the right decision about any other weapons when we get there. I can make no other promises."

Diego tried to rest, but anxiety and all the 'what ifs' a mission brought kept him from sleeping as soundly as he would have liked.

They would start just before sunset and make the trip in less than a night. Diego stared at the rough-hewn ceiling for a while, trying to remember the ship when he had been in it before. Treela would be invaluable in this operation. The unknown factor was her father. What if he was there? What if they had to deal with prisoners on the trip?

He rolled over, facing the wall, trying to will all the unknowns out of his mind. Apparently, he must have fallen asleep because a bright light woke him up. Diego jerked up and wiped the sleep out of his eyes. There had been no dreams, good or bad. He counted that as a plus.

Tellis stood in the doorway. "It is time for us to go."

"I'll be right out."

"Very well." The Trolog left.

Diego washed his face and as much of his body as he could using the underground water that trickled into the basin on one side of the cubicle. The cold water woke him up. He slipped on his environmental suit, minus the helmet and fins. Then he stepped past the cloth door covering providing privacy in the underground city. Tellis was waiting, and Diego followed him to the eating place. All two dozen Trologs were there, plus Storeem.

On a table near one wall, an assortment of quick-to-eat food items awaited. Diego chose a selection of provisions to fuel him through their nocturnal journey.

Tellis led with Diego right behind him. It impressed Diego at how organized they were. The assault force carried their equipment in backpacks, which he knew were heavy, but the Trologs carried them as though they weighed nothing. He felt his pack banging against his back with every step. His admiration grew for these people of such a blasted land.

It did not surprise him when they arrived almost two hours before sunrise. Despite being winded, they went to the surveillance position. Fress and Rreengrol were there. Treela came out as soon as Diego showed up. He could tell she was keyed up.

"They have been working hard, loading supplies into the ship," she said.

"Has your father shown up yet?"

Treela paused before answering. "If he has, I haven't been able to see him."

"Our ambition is to take the ship, not kill those on board," Diego reassured her. "Will it bother you if someone gets hurt or..."

"Killed? Of course, it will. Will it change my mind on what needs to be done? No." She pulled in a shaky breath. "Please try not to hurt my father, though."

"Of course. We're not planning on hurting anyone."

CHAPTER FORTY

"What is the plan?" Rreengrol asked, changing the subject.

Diego outlined what they were going to do. Tendar and Storeem joined them.

"The assault force will go down first and get into position. You and your crew members will join them. The means you have for detecting any who are not a part of this expedition, please employ it," Storeem said. "I will come down half an hour after the first group."

"According to Treela, the ship has a weight allowance for twenty crewmembers," Diego reminded them. "If there are any aboard that we can't get off, then some members of this group will have to stay behind."

"Of course. We do not want to fail before we even start," Storeem said.

"Most of my men will stay behind anyway once the ship is ours." Tendar pulled a bramble off his cloak. "Unless there are more casualties than expected."

"Let's hope not." Diego watched the red sun begin its fiery journey. The early morning coolness was already gone.

"We need to go." Without another word, Tendar set off, motioning the others to follow him. The dozen descended the path in eerie silence, and Diego tried to follow their example. Rreengrol and Fress were near the end of the line. He didn't hear them either. The sun already radiated heat off the rocks.

A quick look at the valley showed very few people out. The last workers headed through the door of their shelter. The ship's hatch was closed on the near side. He would check out the emergency hatch farther down the vessel.

The group reached the valley floor. Tendar checked out their route to the ship. Most of the pallets, piles, and stacks were gone, he assumed, stored on the ship. Diego couldn't help but think they were being watched. *Fress?*

We are being watched from the ship. An individual is monitoring our progress.

What?

I only feel one. Others — a few — are getting ready for sleep.

Diego relayed the information to Tendar.

The Trolog scratched behind his ear. "We still must try. If it's a trap, then we should be able to overcome them." Tendar gazed at him. "How do you know this?"

"I would like to keep one secret."

"It's a good secret to keep. Let's go."

They crept toward the ship. Tendar separated the outlanders and led a few to the main hatch. He motioned Diego to the hatch on the other side of the ship. He, Rreengrol, and Fress, along with the five Trologs accompanying them, trotted to the other hatch. The hatch was shut but not sealed. That would have raised red flags even without Fress's ability.

"There are several inside this hatch," she whispered.

"Let's see how tough they are," Rreengrol whispered back. He passed the information back to the others.

Diego pulled open the hatch and felt the heat of a laser weapon. Thankfully, it didn't hit anyone, and he leaped in, rolling on the floor, his stun-stick out. A bit-off howl and then a moan told him he had connected.

I think they suspected something because there are no sleepers. All are down here. A few are in the control room.

How many?

Hard to tell. About a half dozen.

Then we need to get there. We can't wait for the others to get ambushed somewhere else.

I remember the way, Fress said.

"Tendar, we are going to take the control room."

The Trolog made a motion that he had understood him.

Diego, Rreengrol, Fress, and one of the Trolog outlanders ran down the corridor, meeting no one until they got to the elevator leading to the control room. Diego paused. "Wouldn't they figure out what's going on if we use the elevator?"

"Yes," Rreengrol answered. "They probably have someone waiting by the door to either kill or capture us."

"The one by the door doesn't care which," Fress stated. The Trolog stared at her.

"Is there an access ladder?" Diego asked, remembering his climb up the access ladder on *Star Devourer* that he and the Turengen had used the previous year. "Several of us can go that way, and the rest of you use the elevator. Wait a few minutes to allow us to climb to the upper level."

"Yes," Fress said with a chitter. "Follow me." Diego, Rreengrol, and a smaller-built outlander followed her.

She led them to a small door that wasn't meant to slide open. Diego felt along the edges and found a small latch. He pulled at it and then pushed. With a sigh, the door opened inward, revealing a narrow metal ladder.

"Let me go first. Smaller."

Diego nodded to the Turengen. She had to reach for the rungs, but it didn't slow her down. He followed right behind her, feeling the ladder in the pitch dark. Cobwebs and dust coated all of them. It seemed today's space voyagers didn't know about this access. How Fress had found it, he didn't know. When they reached the top, she pulled the door open toward her. Despite the door being smaller than the one below, Fress slipped through the entrance before it fully opened.

Diego bent until he was on his hands and knees, and then he slid into the control room. Treela's father was in the captain's chair in front of him while two of the crew were waiting and watching by the elevator door. The controls were lit up, showing the elevator was rising.

None of the Trologs heard or saw the four who slipped in from the emergency access. "Now!" Diego hissed. Racing toward Captain Tremorin, Diego bore him to the ground before Treela's father even knew he was there. There was a flash that sizzled on the deck, but the Trolog and Rreengrol overpowered the two by the elevator, stunning them into submission. Wrenching the pistol out of the captain's hand, Diego held it at the Trolog's head. "I would like for this to be a peaceful takeover," he said, waiting a second for the translator to do its job.

The elevator door opened to show them an outlander. He saw the scene and grinned. "Do you need me?"

"We will. And thanks for distracting them."

"What are you going to do now? You don't have the code for running the ship," Tremorin said with a sneer. "And I already started the sequence."

Fress trotted to the navigational computer, using the shorter stun stick to force the helmsman out of his seat. She jumped up and began tapping on the keyboard. She could get the code from someone's head. "Do you want me to speed up the sequence and get us out of here, Commander?"

"Yes, let's do it!"

"What? How?" Tremorin blustered.

"Grab onto something if you aren't in a seat," Rreengrol shouted, jerking the second helmsman out of his seat and sliding in and buckling himself up.

The outland Trologs buckled themselves in.

Diego slid into the command chair even as the ship rumbled, then shuddered. Captain Tremorin grabbed a seat and buckled himself in. Diego found the controls for communications. "Take off. Strap yourselves in. Imminent take off!"

Diego located the straps and secured himself in as the engines roared. It ascended, slowly at first, then with increasing speed, shoving them into their seats or against the hard floor. "Monitors."

Fress activated the forward monitor, and they watched as the reddish sky changed to more purple, then black. The screen toned down the sun as the predetermined course took the Trolog ship through its system and toward the gate to Amashi. An unconscious Trolog floated from the deck.

Rreengrol put the ship into a gravitational spin that wasn't a full gravity but allowed them to get around normally.

Captain Tremorin groaned and unstrapped himself. "I will kill you with my bare hands."

"No, you won't." He motioned to the Trolog outlander. "Can you and Rreengrol take these five to a safe place where you can lock them up?"

"Yes, Captain."

"And if you find Tendar and the others, have him send a couple of his men up here."

"Yes, sir."

Diego sighed as soon as the group left. "That was too easy," he muttered.

"Maybe, but we are heading to Amashi," Fress replied. "When we are in the system, we will resolve any other problems."

"If you can, check out the flight sequence and make sure there aren't any surprise detours. We'll need to check the cargo for weaponry."

Diego pondered the course Fress put up on his computer screen and studied the placement of the portals. The one closest to Amashi was exactly where they had found it before when they were accompanying the Trolog ship. The one nearest to Trolog was outside of their solar system. Over two days. "Getting the coordinates of these portals for a return trip, Fress?"

"Yes, sir."

Rreengrol and several outlanders, including Tendar, came up the elevator. Diego didn't realize they were there until the door whooshed opened. He jerked up, startled. He had been so intent he hadn't heard a thing.

"I knew who was coming, Commander," Fress mentioned.

"That's a bad habit, you know."

Fress chittered. "Let me know when it is bothering you too much."

"No, just teasing. When it concerns a mission or crew welfare, I can't be upset."

"We have them locked in several cabins. The captain is locked up by himself," Rreengrol reported.

"Good. I want Tendar to take command while you and I check the cargo."

The Grrlock unstrapped himself. "Figuring on any surprises?"

Diego just motioned to Rreengrol to follow him, and then he stopped and turned back. "Tendar, how many men do you have in various parts of the ship?"

"Two guard the prisoners, two others watch the elevators, and I sent five who are off duty and presumably sleeping."

"Good idea. When we get back, perhaps you should get some sleep, too. I want you in command any time I'm not up here."

"Yes, sir. And do not forget to rest." He smiled. "By the way, the captain said the trip will be over in a little over three days."

"Yes, we need to monitor the systems and hull integrity for those several days." He and Rreengrol entered the elevator.

"I don't know what to expect, but if this ship isn't going much farther than Amashi, then why so much in the way of cargo?"

"That's a good question, Diego."

They met an outlander at the elevator entrance. The man saluted, almost in the fashion of the soldiers of California. Diego saluted back. When they had walked halfway through the ship, they took an elevator down to the cargo. An outlander stood guard at that elevator as well. The lights were dim, but they brightened as the two entered. Crates and boxes were stacked and fastened down. Rreengrol climbed to the top of one pile and tried to decipher the writing. He opened one box and pulled out a long rod with a bulbous end.

"There's a bunch of these in here, but I don't know what they are, Diego."

Diego climbed up on another stack and opened the top box. When he pushed aside the wadded cushioning, he pulled out a glowing ball about the size of his two hands put together. There were several more in the box. "What in the world is this thing?" It almost appeared delicate, like glass.

Rreengrol peered in beside him. He gazed at the globe in Diego's hands. His green eyes looked troubled. "I think you'd better put it back. We should have Fress with us when we talk to the prisoners."

"All right, so what's bothering you?"

"I don't think these are trade goods, Diego. There is something about those globes that has me worried. Not sure why. They give me a funny feeling."

Diego carefully put the globe back, replacing the material that cushioned it. He put the lid back. They checked several other boxes and crates and found other things unfamiliar to them. In fact, when they left the cargo hold, Diego realized there had not been one thing that was for the sustenance of the crew. No food, no comfort items, like bedding or medical supplies, nothing he felt people like himself might want on a voyage to another planet.

"Let's go get Fress and Tendar. You'll take command

while we're questioning the captain."

Rreengrol nodded. They headed back to the control room in silence. Diego could only think the Dominar had something nasty stored in the cargo hold.

Tendar got up from the command chair, and Rreengrol took his place. "Fress, is the heading on automatic?"

"Yes, sir."

"Good. I would like you and Tendar to accompany me to the crew's quarters. Commander Rreengrol will assume command while we're gone." He beckoned them to follow him. In the elevator, he explained. "There are some unknowns in the cargo hold I want to question the captured crew about. First, though, Tendar, I'd like you to look at a couple of things. You might recognize what they are."

"Of course."

Again, they made their way down to the hold. Tendar's breath hissed between his teeth when he saw the globes.

"What are they?"

"I don't know for sure, but there was an old rhyme that told of a ball of fire." He reached out as though to touch the globe, but his hand stopped a few inches above it.

Diego could see the glow through his hand.

"In the brightest day,
I came to play,
With my little ball so round,
The sun grew dark,
The trees and the park,
All hid beneath the ground,
I saw my bones rattle and play.
They melted away.
Afraid of my ball of fire."

CHAPTER FORTY-ONE

The guard unlocked the captain's cabin. The door slid open, showing Diego an almost totally dark room. Tendar pushed a button, but nothing happened—no light came on. He pulled a small, round device out of his pocket and pushed on it. Light pulsed from the object.

Diego glanced at Fress.

"He is here." She trotted over to an open locker and jerked down a uniform. Captain Tremorin crouched in the back, holding a tapering rod in front of him like a knife. He didn't move.

"We need to talk to you about what's in your cargo bay," Diego said, sitting on the end of the narrow bunk.

Tremorin glared at each of them. "I have no intention of talking to you. You turned my daughter away from me."

Diego shook his head. "Your Dominar did that. Treela was in the second group that was going to help take this ship. We didn't need that group, so she is back on Trolog, worrying about you."

The captain flew out of the locker faster than anyone thought possible. He tackled Diego, stabbing the point of the rod into the fleshy part of his upper arm. "¡Madre de Dios!" The pain radiated up his arm, bringing sudden tears to his eyes.

Tendar jerked Tremorin away and shoved him into the one small chair in the room, grabbing the rod away from him.

Fress snatched a towel in the captain's bathroom while Diego unfastened the sleeve of his environmental suit. The Turengen pressed the towel to the wound.

"Just bind it until we finish here," Diego said. He ignored the pain as he turned his attention to Tremorin. "The supplies in your cargo hold aren't trade goods. Especially the rods with the funny-looking bulbous ends."

Tremorin stared at him, his eyes widening. Diego didn't need Fress's confirmation to tell him those items were familiar to the captain.

Diego continued, "And the bright golden globes — the ones that look like they have a powerful light source inside. They're some kind of weapon, aren't they?"

Tremorin gaped at him. "These were in the cargo hold?"

"You didn't know what cargo they stored in your ship?" Diego held still while Fress tied the cloth around his wound.

"They loaded it under the Dominar's orders. They sealed everything." Sweat popped out on Tremorin's forehead.

Diego thought for a moment. What did the Dominar have in mind? "Tell me your orders, Captain. We have lethal weapons on board this ship. Are we part of a plan to destroy an entire civilization and to be killed doing it? We're all in a dangerous position, and the only way out of it is to cooperate."

Tremorin took a deep breath, stared at Diego, and then bowed his head. His voice was low, and Diego had to lean forward to hear him. "The Dominar told me he decided to negotiate with the water planet people. He told me he had trade goods in the hold that he hoped would appeal to them."

Diego continued pressing for information. "What did I describe to you, Captain Tremorin?"

"They are components of the device we were looking for on that water planet."

"So, you found what you were looking for."

"Apparently, we did. I suspect the scientists learned how to reconstruct them."

"Explain what you mean by that. You didn't know what you found on the Amashi world?"

"The Dominar's scientists had found most of the plans to

build the weapon. They just didn't have the means to set it off. That's why we were there when you discovered us. I don't know if I found something on the planet or if the scientists figured out how to explode it. I wasn't told."

"It appears the device is in pieces," Diego began. "Is there someone here who is supposed to put it together?"

"There is only my crew on board. None of the scientists came aboard with us. If someone was assigned to assemble it, he or she isn't on board. And if it's supposed to detonate, I can only suppose they already set the device. Probably, it's computerized. The scientists worked on board the ship for the past several days. I am not a scientist, so I don't know how the device works."

Diego jumped up. "*Santa Maria!* We are sitting on a weapon of immeasurable power, and none of us have a clue how it works or how to stop it from detonating. The outland scientists were part of the second group coming down the mountain. They could have figured it all out."

Tremorin took a deep breath. "We knew there were outlanders in the mountains. You were to be captured when you tried to take the ship, but when you came during the day, that ruined our plans."

Diego felt his anger rising but now wasn't the time. "So, this was all about the Dominar getting revenge."

Tremorin growled. "Apparently"

"Would there have been anyone in your crew who might know the actual plan?" Diego asked.

"I don't think so."

"Captain Tremorin, they have betrayed you. The Dominar never considered trading. He kept you ignorant of his actual plans. You and your crew are being sacrificed to satisfy his desire for revenge and conquest." Diego paused. "Can we count on you to work with us to save your crew and the lives of millions on a planet that had nothing to do with your people's problems?"

The Trolog captain nodded. "Yes. I was angry when I read the history, and I blamed the people who lived in the ocean. My daughter tried to read some of the old records to me, but I denied the truth. It frustrated me when I realized the ancients brought their destruction on themselves. I remember discussing this with the Dominar and being relieved when he agreed with me. Yes, I will work with you. I don't know what I can do, but I will try to save lives."

"Thank you."

"Be aware, this ship is on a set course. That's why there are so few of us. The scientists said it was only necessary to make sure the course stayed constant until we reached the Amashi system. The Dominar mentioned our technology might interest the Amashi."

Diego snorted. "The Seressin might be interested, except they already have those kinds of navigational computers. The Amashi couldn't care less. They are only interested in living peacefully in their oceans."

Tremorin said nothing for a few moments. "I want to check out the cargo hold to make an identification of what's down there."

"By all means. I will join you, Fress, and Tendar, as soon as I get this bound up."

Tendar spoke up. "I will have one of my men join us and then stand guard over the cargo. It will be a while before we reach the gate, and if there is the possibility someone could be the Dominar's agent...."

"That's wise, Tendar." Diego held out his injured arm. "This isn't too bad, so it shouldn't take long."

On his way to the medical bay, Diego found an outlander to help him. They pulled out the supplies needed to clean and bind his wound. The weapon caused pain, but it had fractured no bones. He contacted Rreengrol and let him know their location and what was going on.

Fress, I know it will be difficult, but can you listen in on conversations? Just in case one of the Dominar's agents is on board.

It's getting easier to read these people's minds. The captain is as surprised about this development as we were.

"Ow! ¡Pico!" Diego cried out. "What did you put on that?" The outlander had sprayed something on his arm and was wiping away the blood. The Trolog picked up another bottle, sprayed something else, and the pain ceased. Diego thought the numbing spray should have been first. He returned to the conversation with Fress. *I thought he was. I just wish I could figure out how this is supposed to happen, especially if no one is on board to move this plot along.*

Could the secret be in the computers? she asked.

It could, but you can't be in more than one place at a time.

Finding the information is more important than spying on people, she reminded him.

You are right. The science computer would be the first place to check.

Let me begin now, with your permission.

Go ahead. The Trolog finished binding his arm, and Diego headed to the cargo hold at a trot.

"Your little crewmember left a few minutes ago. She didn't tell me where she was going," Tremorin informed him.

"It's possible the secret to detonating all of this is in the computers. Fress is one of my best crew members on a computer. If there is anything stored in them, she'll find it."

As Diego expected, Captain Tremorin identified the crates as components of the monster weapon of their past.

"Why don't we send the cargo out the airlock?" Tendar ventured.

"We need to think this through." Diego stood next to the large container holding the golden globes. "I can't imagine there wouldn't be safeguards on these crates and boxes. Are the globes the power source?"

"I believe so," Tremorin replied. "One of the Dominar's scientists showed me a huge metal device, like a crucible, round with thick plates on the outside and a tiny window on one side. It glowed. He said the glow represented an immense power they could store in small, glass-like globes. Each one, he told me, would contain enough power to blow up our city. I asked him why we would want to blow up our city. The ancients had already done that. The scientist laughed and said we could destroy our enemies' cities."

"You knew they had all the information?" Diego asked.

"No. He told me they had only portions of the weapon. There was a part of me, even then, that wished they would never find the rest. I pushed the conversation out of my mind."

"So, you don't think we could send them into space?" Tendar wondered.

Diego rubbed his chin. "No. If these components are all controlled by the computer, perhaps the computer could control a globe in the airlock or just outside the ship. Besides, who do we ask to go in the airlock to release one globe?"

No one said anything for several seconds.

You are correct, Commander. I need time to study the computer system. Fress had been listening to the conversation.

"We're going to let Fress study the computer as long as we can. Hopefully, she'll find something that will help us."

Tremorin stood nearby. "Commander, you asked about my crew. I think I need to talk to them. If the crew believes me and remembers their oath of service, we can trust them. If any of them are uncomfortable helping us, then I'll know, and we can lock them in their cabins."

"That's an acceptable plan, too. Tendar, go with him."

"Of course, Commander."

Diego figured he might as well go back to the control room. He wasn't doing any good in the cargo hold, and any ideas floating in his mind could probably fit in his mother's thimble.

When the elevator door opened, Rreengrol slid out of the captain's chair and into the weaponry officer's seat. "The ship is on course toward the first portal."

Diego relayed everything Tremorin had told him.

"So, we are on a course to destroy Amashi," Rreengrol replied.

The other Trolog crew members gazed at them with large, frightened eyes. If any of them were agents of the Dominar, they were also excellent actors, Diego thought. He glanced at Fress working at the main computer.

She looked up at him and shook her head. *They are all surprised. And so far, I have found nothing to refute Rreengrol's statement.* She bent back over the computer.

CHAPTER FORTY-TWO

Several hours later, when Captain Tremorin entered the control room, Diego didn't relinquish the command chair. "How many of your crew will work with us?"

"All but two. I locked them in separate cabins."

"Good. But just to be on the safe side, have Tendar's outlanders assigned to monitor your other crew members. Just in case someone is hiding their affiliation with the Dominar. Right now, we need to figure out how we are going to keep this ship from its rendezvous. Have you found anything, Fress?"

"I have discovered the program running the ship, but I couldn't alter its course."

"What else do the computers control? Weapons? Life support? I want to know everything this ship is going to do."

"It will take a little while, Commander."

"Take your time, Fress. Within reason, that is." Diego had studied a great deal in the past almost two years, but he couldn't think of anything to help them. He wondered if they could control the engine speed. Could they stop? "Stop all engines," he ordered. The helmsmen pushed the right buttons, but Diego still felt the engine vibrations.

"The system isn't complying, sir."

"I'm not surprised."

Fress cut into his thoughts. "I think I understand. When the program was loaded onto the ship's computer, it took over all functions like navigation and the engines. The computer warned me when I tried to hack into the program. I have discovered that when we go through the first portal, the engines will accelerate. When we enter the second gate, the computer will signal all the components. When we are within a set range of either the planet or its sun, the components will explode."

Again, Diego tried to think of something but couldn't. It sounded like a perfect plot.

"Could we disable the engines manually in the engine room?" Tremorin asked. "I have had experience with this ship's engines."

"I doubt it." Fress referred to the computer. After a few minutes, she turned back. "The computer also has control over life support systems. It could kill us and then continue the mission."

"What if we sent a crate out of the hatch?" Rreengrol suggested.

"That wouldn't happen. Each crate and component have wireless connections with the computer." Fress chittered her frustration. "I am trying to break into this program, but I haven't figured it out yet."

"Maybe if I helped?" the Trolog helmsman asked. "I've worked on computers for years. I came to make sure this computer didn't have any problems." She gave a sarcastic laugh.

"What's your name?" Diego asked.

"Lieutenant Trilenn," the young woman said.

"If you two can figure out a way out of our current mess, I sure don't mind."

"Don't mind either," Fress concurred. She motioned for the Trolog to join her. They began talking about computers as fast as the translator could handle it.

Tendar had joined them and was standing as quietly as a shadow. Diego turned to him. "I think we need to make a walk-through inspection of the ship. Captain Tremorin, can you join us? Maybe if we examine everything, something — anything — might occur to us. Rreengrol, you are in charge again. Let me know when we're close to the portal."

"All right, Commander."

They were silent in the elevator. A guard saluted when they exited.

Small ideas began flitting through Diego's mind. "Captain, the ship appeared to be one long tube with several attached levels."

"Yes. The Control Room is at the top level of the forward compartment."

"I have wondered why there are no escape pods. Has that always been a feature of your spacecraft?" Even ships from his home world had boats the sailors could lower away from a stricken man-o-war.

Tremorin shook his head. "And to think I had my daughter with me on the last flight." He gazed at Diego for a moment. "When they refurbished this ship, they added an escape craft. However, the government decided that since this was the only spacecraft, if any disaster happened, there would be no one to come to the rescue. We changed the pod for the scientific equipment, allowing the ship to go below the surface of the water. I wonder if the Dominar had this in mind all along?"

In the cargo hold, Diego gazed at the schematics on the computer. "You said the scientists created this ship from the remains of other spacecraft?"

"Yes."

Diego rubbed behind his ear. If the ship was cobbled together, why couldn't it be taken apart? "Let's go aft."

The engine room was immense and noisy. This must have been a monumental task, putting together something to power the ship in space and underwater. He said as much to Tremorin and Tendar. "You know that kind of technology might be worth something to the Seressin."

"If we live long enough to see if they're interested."

"Of course," Diego agreed. "Still, it's a fascinating concept."

They only spent a few minutes in the living quarters.

"I can't think of a thing we could try to prevent the ship from doing exactly what it's programmed to do," Tremorin said.

Again, Diego studied the bulkhead.

"What are you thinking, Commander?" Tendar asked.

"Is there equipment on board we could use to take the ship apart?"

"What! Why?"

Diego continued. "It depends on whether we can maintain life support in the forward section."

Tendar just stood with his mouth hanging open.

"Life support, propulsion...."

Diego mused out loud. "I don't think propulsion will be as big an issue. If we can contact someone in the Seressin Empire...."

Tremorin scowled. "We can't contact anyone except on Trolog."

"I assumed that. I believe we can overcome that problem."

"How many missions have you led?" Tremorin asked.

Diego felt frustrated that his thoughts weren't as easy to explain as he would have liked. He needed to discuss his ideas with Fress and Rreengrol. "Probably as many as you have, Captain, if what you are saying is true," he snapped. "How many times has this ship gone into space since it was created?" Diego reined in his feelings. "I'm sorry. To you, I suppose I am a child. The Dominar thought I was, but I have led two sanctioned missions and two unsanctioned missions. I am still learning, and sometimes I feel stupid considering that the world I came from didn't have computers or spaceships."

Tremorin sighed. "I am sorry, too, but you aren't that much older than my daughter."

"I am almost sixteen and often wish I was still on my home planet, riding horses and branding cattle. It's simple work compared to this. I have an idea, but I want to discuss this with my two crew members. They are the first to let me know if what I propose is too far afield."

Tremorin smiled. "Fair enough. I am assuming what you want to do will take place between the gates?"

"Yes. If it's possible."

"Can Lieutenant Trell join you? He is the most talented engineering mind on this ship."

"I would welcome his help," Diego said, thinking Fress would discern if Trell was one of the Dominar's men.

They returned to the control room together. Diego left Tremorin in charge and took Fress, Rreengrol, and Trell into the captain's ready room just off the control room. Diego pulled up the ship's schematics on his computer and looked through them to see if they matched what he had seen in the cargo hold.

"You have something bizarre and outrageous in mind. I can tell," Rreengrol muttered, but he turned on his computer as did the other two.

Thankfully, Fress said nothing, although Diego felt he was as transparent as his mother's crystal glassware. "You're right," he said with a tired smile. "Trell, you have the most experience with this ship. Captain Tremorin told me the scientists created it from the remains of several spaceships. I was fortunate enough to see the Seressin shipyards about a year ago. I watched as robots and technicians took apart decommissioned ships and repaired ships that had been in battle. Is there any equipment for fixing breaches on this ship? Robots that can go out into space to do repairs?"

Trell shrugged. "Yes. We have six cutters and low-G fabricators. We don't have any robots."

"Would your machinery be able to cut this ship apart?"

"What?" The Trolog's green eyes grew large. "While we are traveling in space?"

"I was right," Rreengrol said with a sigh. "It is bizarre."

"Yes. Do we have spacesuits for everyone?"

"There were only supposed to be twenty crewmembers, although we've had more," the Trolog said. "I'll check that out. Of course, if we worked on a compartment at a time, then everyone doesn't need to be wearing a suit simultaneously."

Diego frowned. "That's taking quite a chance, though. If we have enough suits, how long would it take to detach the forward section from the rest of the ship? From the schematics, I notice they fitted the entire forward section of the ship *Star Wanderer* onto the body of the *Starfire Cruiser*."

"Yes, and the engines came from *Far Star*."

"What is the name of this ship?" Diego asked, almost embarrassed that he hadn't even thought about that.

"*Revenge*."

"So that was the primary purpose from the beginning."

"I guess. I know the Dominar blamed the ancients' enemies every time someone protested about some shortage." Trell rubbed his chin. "As to your question of time, if all six machines were used to take off the forward section, it would probably take...." Trell punched in some numbers, looked at the screen, and punched in some more numbers. "Two days and that's only if we use the machines the entire time. However, I am not sure the machines have enough power to run that long."

CHAPTER FORTY-THREE

Diego paced away from the others and then turned back. "What kind of power do they use? The same thing the engines use?"

"Yes," Trell said.

"Would there be a way to use the engine's power source to power the cutters?" Diego asked.

"It's a closed system, Commander," Fress interjected. "So most likely, no."

Diego sat back and thought.

"What about those fancy globes?" Rreengrol asked.

Diego grinned at his friend and then turned to Trell and Fress. "Is that workable?"

"The power is the same, but whether we could harness it, I don't know," Trell replied as he continued studying his computer. "There may be a way to adapt the machines to using the globe fuel, but that's only if the program will allow it."

"Why don't we inventory the spacesuits first and then have six capable crewmembers start the separation," Diego said.

"Could we continue to work in here when we need to, Commander?" Fress asked.

"I want you two, along with Trilenn, to continue working out all the issues together. At least here, it's a little quieter. Consider this your workroom." Diego got up. "I forgot an obvious question. Is there enough room in the forward section for all the crew to fit when we separate?"

Trell replied, "Yes, it will be crowded, but we can make it. And Commander Rreengrol is correct. This is bizarre."

Rreengrol just gave a purring laugh and slapped Diego on the shoulder.

Diego called Captain Tremorin. and Tendar and explained the plans to them. To his credit, the captain didn't protest too much. He just shrugged and then said, "I will have crewmembers find all available suits and select the best crew to start the cutting."

"Good! And Trilenn and Fress also calculate the reaction of the engine when the front end is gone. Trajectories, speeds, and so on."

"Yes, Commander," Fress chittered. She retrieved Trilenn from the control room, and the trio trotted back to their computers.

"And Captain?"

"Yes, Commander."

"What about the feasibility of adapting those power globes to the machines?"

"I wouldn't suggest it," Tremorin replied. "However, I think the weapons locker has a container with power modules that would fit the cutters. We could extend the two days to three with the extra energy cartridges."

"That's great news. Thanks, Captain! Gentlemen, let's leave these three alone so they can solve the problems of the galaxy. We need to get busy. I don't think we have much time."

Regardless, Diego stayed behind when the others left. "Fress, I want you to be honest with me about this idea. Is it workable?" While none of the others had voiced any strong objections, he saw doubt in their eyes, and it made him question his plan.

"Commander, if I had not thought this had any chance of working, I would have said so. It will not be easy, but I can think of nothing else."

"Thanks, Fress. Carry on." He left and sat down in the command chair. Diego pulled up the ship's schematics on the computer.

"For what it's worth, I hope this works," Rreengrol said with a laugh. "How are we going to make our way through space without engines?"

"Look at this." Diego began drawing on the computer screen. His rendition of the ship was simple. He added some more things, erased, and drew more, including his best vision of a portal. When he finished, he studied Rreengrol's face.

His friend nodded. "So, if we time it right, then we will go through the gate to Amashi while the rest of the ship continues on in the void between systems."

"Yes. That means if it explodes, then it will harm no one. And if it doesn't explode, then there is time for a Seressin battlecruiser to find and destroy it later."

"By my dam's whiskers, you aren't making anything easy, are you?"

"There is nothing easy about this," Diego replied. "The only unknown is the computer."

Rreengrol waved his hand at the drawing. "Where in the world did you get this idea?"

Diego shrugged. "Where I grew up, salvaging and reusing things were common. Some things were too rare to just toss away, especially in the colonies. When Tremorin mentioned how they had cobbled together the ship from the parts of old ships, it made me wonder why we couldn't take it apart."

"Except we're in space."

"Yes, we are."

"I just hope we have enough spacesuits."

"If not, then we'll just have to be more careful."

Rreengrol snorted.

CHAPTER FORTY-FOUR

"We have enough suits for everyone onboard," Tendar reported.

Diego considered Tendar's news to be one of the few bits of luck in this entire bizarre mission. He sent several of the crew to make sure each air tank contained enough oxygen. When each of them found a suit that fit, they took it with them to their sleeping quarters. Diego picked out the smallest for Fress and two he thought Trilenn and Trell could wear. When he looked for one that fit him, Diego found he had a suit almost a foot too tall for him. While he didn't consider himself short, this suit belonged to a very tall Trolog.

One crewmember modified the welding equipment to become cutters as well. The cutting was done with one man outside the ship working, and then another working on the inside. They kept hatches closed to conserve air in areas not affected by the 'decapitation of the ship,' as the crew began calling it.

"We have less than a day before we reach the first portal," a helmsman reported.

"How is our progress?" Diego asked.

"One third completed."

Diego nodded. "Are the modifications to communications complete? Will we be able to send a message to nearby Seressin ships?"

"Yes, sir."

"Good. Make sure all necessary supplies and equipment are brought forward before our first jump."

By the time the first portal passage was imminent, everyone had donned their spacesuits. They used the cutters until the last second before the gut-wrenching passage through the portal.

Diego sucked in a deep breath. He heard the rumble of engines firing.

"Ship is accelerating," a helmsman called out.

It wasn't unexpected. "I doubt it's going to have any effect, but see if you can bring the engines to half speed."

The helmsman shook his head. "No good, Commander."

"Get the crews working on the cutting!" Diego ordered.

The crew members worked in two-hour shifts. The cutters began looking ragged.

Diego was sure they would not have the job finished by the time they reached the other portal. "How soon to the next gate?"

"Another day," Trilenn informed him. She gazed at him, her eyes large.

"Are you going to make that rendezvous you carved out for yourself?" the captain asked.

"We have to," Diego said through tight lips.

Donning his too-large spacesuit, he checked on the cutters who were working on the inside of the ship. None were outside. Even though whoever was out there would travel at the same speed as the ship, tethers wouldn't help if someone lost their grip. There was also the problem of losing the equipment. Diego hated the equipment being put in the same category as the lives of the crew, but losing even one cutter would make the goal impossible to reach.

At first, Diego watched in person, pacing from room to room, until Rreengrol reminded him he was allowing air to escape, so he watched on monitors. He felt so tired; he dozed in the captain's chair. Diego gave Rreengrol the con and headed into the meeting room where Fress and Trilenn were still working.

"The couch is adequate," Fress said without preamble.

"Just for a few minutes. Wake me up in a little while."

"We have eight hours," she reminded him.

Diego yawned. "Don't let me sleep more than a few hours."
He didn't remember stretching out. He did remember the dream!

*They had almost separated the ship. Cutters sliced at some
of the last seams. A huge distortion showed up in the distance. The
portal! Diego didn't realize the space anomalies were so large. And they
wouldn't make it. The globes! They could help.*

*Diego ran down the corridor and into the cargo hold. He skidded
to a halt, trying to peer through the darkness. They had cut the power to
the unnecessary rooms in the aft part of the ship. Pulling out a flashlight,
he found the crate containing the long rods with smaller versions of
globes on the end.*

*Trilenn was behind him, calling out. "I think the Dominar
gathered all weapons, great and small, to make the ship one immense
explosive device."*

"What are these?" Why hadn't anyone told him this earlier?

*"They are the portable version of the larger globes. They were
going to be used against the outlanders, but this project became more
important to him."*

"Can the small globes come off?"

"I don't know. I will examine a projectile and see."

"Be careful," Diego admonished her.

*Trilenn studied the rod and then pushed a button. She and
the rest of the room exploded in a fiery ball of fire, engulfing him and
traveling through the entire ship, gaining power as it went.*

Diego jerked up and shook his head. Trilenn and Fress
were gazing at him, their faces worried.

"Are you all right, Commander?" Fress asked.

"Yes." Diego remembered the dream and realized the
weapons might be the key, but the trick was using them so they
didn't kill anyone else. "Did you see any of it?"

"Fire. Much fire and death," Fress replied. Trilenn stared
at her, her mouth open.

"Yes, Trilenn, Fress, and her people have a fair amount of

telepathic ability," Diego explained. "And I have the reputation for dreaming of the future, and sometimes the foretelling allows me to avoid some consequences."

"Was this a foretelling?"

Diego nodded. "I'm pretty sure it was. How long was I asleep?"

"Two hours," Fress told him. *In your dream, I saw Trilenn die.*

You saw all of us die, Fress. That stopped the destruction of Amashi and the Amashina, but I want more. I want to not only save them but save us, too.

I would like that. Fress thought.

"The cargo hold has the answer," Diego said.

"Then maybe we should go there and hope the answers come to you," Fress told him.

Diego repeated the telepathic conversation with Trilenn.

"It's worth the attempt," the Trolog replied.

Diego felt a quick twinge at the images from his recent dream. "We have little time. Let's do it now."

Tendar was in the control room. Diego motioned for him to come with them. "Rreengrol, you're in charge. Captain Tremorin, we're going to need your help."

They trotted through the corridors in silence, seeing no one. Either everyone was in the lower rooms of the forward section, on the cutting crew, or in the control room.

Tremorin sucked in his breath when they entered the cargo hold. There was a glow from several of the crates. The navigational program was priming the weapons for their assault on Amashi.

"Captain," Diego said as he opened the crate with the rods. "These are smaller personal arms, aren't they? Made for soldiers to shoot each other?"

"Yes, but who told you that?"

"It came to me. I will explain how later." Diego felt nervous energy coursing through his body.

"They are deadly. What did you have in mind, Commander?"

"We will not have enough time to finish with the cutters."

"You aren't proposing to use these weapons, are you?" Tremorin looked at Diego as though he were a madman.

"Yes. It will be close. I have seen the progress, and I don't think it would take a lot of force to blow the last welds. That's all that will hold this ship together—some very good welding."

"So, when do you plan on doing this, Commander?" Tendar asked. "There is still more cutting to do."

"We take four weapons. By the time we are close to the portal, only four spots will have the two sections of the ship attached. Just before we reach the portal, we will station someone at each of those places anchored to the bow section. They will shoot their weapons at the welds. Someone will be in the forward area, ready to pull them in."

"Won't the back of the ship follow us into the portal?" Tremorin asked, looking skeptical.

"I don't think so. The explosion should cause a reaction, pushing the aft section in a different direction."

"Don't forget that the back end has the engines," the Trolog said.

"But not the navigational program it needs to correct course."

Tremorin sighed. "I think the sooner we can do this, the better."

Diego's brain felt as though it raced like a stampede. "The cutters must keep working until the very last second. But as soon as we can, we need to blow this part of the ship away."

"I think we should take more of the personal weapons, maybe six or seven," Tremorin told the group. "That way, if one shot doesn't do it, then two might."

Fress chittered. "That is probably a good idea, as long as the computer program doesn't notice."

Tendar climbed up and pulled out the weapons, handing them down, one at a time. After he had pulled out five, something glowed deep in the box. He put the fifth rod back in, and the glow subsided. "Take those toward the hatch," he instructed.

They did, and Tendar relaxed when the glow didn't reappear. "There seems to be something telling the computer the weapons are being disturbed."

"I agree, Tendar, but let the others take the rods out into the corridor and see if anything happens," Diego suggested.

"You have a communicator," Tendar reminded him. "I will let you know if there are any changes."

The group made it all the way back to the elevator without hearing from Tendar. They locked the weapons in a cabinet on the lower level.

When Tendar arrived, he smiled, the first one Diego had seen since he had met the outlander. "Finally, some luck! Four weapons. We'll have to use the best shots since we only have the four."

Diego breathed a sigh of relief. "We'll check the progress of the work crew and then prepare to finish the job. I will fire one of these...."

Tremorin interrupted and stated, "We have received training."

Diego studied the Trolog captain and agreed that he was right. "All right; you and Tendar."

"And me," Trilenn said. "I have trained on them, too."

Tremorin nodded. "She's right. She's one of our best shots."

Diego knew they were right. "All right. Is there someone else?"

"Yes," Tremorin said. "I will assign Trell down here."

"Make sure you have four strong crew members to pull all of you forward after you have severed the aft section. I don't want to lose anyone. Those who haven't transferred over to the bow section of *Revenge* need to do so now." Diego rode the elevator up to the control room. Every seat had someone sitting in it, with a few seats accommodating two occupants.

He felt someone next to him and looked down to see Fress. "Do you wish me to station myself near Trilenn when she gets ready to break the last weld?" she asked.

"Are you strong enough to pull her in?"

"Turengens are strong. I can pull her in."

Diego nodded. "And you can let me know what's going on down below."

Fress pattered to the elevator. Several Trologs entered the room and were directed to the captain's ready room. Diego didn't doubt a dozen crewmembers had already crowded in there. Everyone wore their suits, with the helmets hanging against their backs.

"One hour to the gate," Rreengrol reported.

"Good." Diego opened his communicator. "How is the separation looking?"

"It's going to be close, Commander," Tendar answered.

"I know." As he ended the communication, a few more Trologs gathered inside the control room. "If it's too crowded in the conference room, then you'll have to stay by the elevator. On the floor," Diego told them.

They squeezed into the smaller room. He thought with sardonic humor that some of them may have to camp out in the bathroom. Six minutes out, the clock on the captain's chair told him. "Regardless of where you're at, drop your cutters. Wait for the shooters," Diego called out to the cutting crew. He got confirmation from all of them, even though he thought he heard someone still working their machine in the background.

"Captain, do you have a clear shot?"

"I think I can make it work."

Diego got almost the same response from the others. "Let me know when all the cutters are away."

There was a minute when he heard nothing, and then Diego perceived the soft clangs and clunks he assumed were the machines being jettisoned. He stared at the monitor, Rreengrol watching over his shoulder, murmuring something in Grrlock. Diego didn't even try to figure out what he said.

"Everyone, seal your helmets. You are on suit air now!" Closer, closer—almost there. Now! "Blow it! Now!"

CHAPTER FORTY-FIVE

The control room normally held six crewmembers, but more than twice that number crowded in there now. Two huddled close to his chair, two more under his computer console, while others were under other consoles or under crewmembers' chairs. A Trolog at the communications panel turned and gazed at him. His pure white hair declared him to be young, maybe younger than Diego. "Commander, were the explosives set to change the direction of the aft section? It won't follow us through the portal, will it?" The Trolog's green eyes were large with fright. Diego couldn't remember the crewman's name, but he understood his fear.

"Yes. They were. We should hear the explosion shortly. And that will send it away from the portal."

Over the communicators, Diego heard the crack and thump of weapon fire. Two fired simultaneously, and right after, the last two fired. Then came another sharp report. That was the weapon to set off the explosives. "Get out of there. Take cover!" Diego hoped Captain Tremorin and his team could hear him.

Diego called out to the crew in the forward area. "Grab on to something! Everybody hang on." He glanced over his shoulder to where Rreengrol stood. "Brace yourself."

Rreengrol clutched the edge of the captain's chair, his claws extended.

They heard a loud boom that didn't need a communicator. The ship rattled, the artificial gravity ceased, then came the dull pulling-apart feeling that accompanied going through a portal. Everything wrenched back to normal except the artificial gravity. Then the lights flickered and went out, leaving only emergency lights glowing a wan orange. With no life support system, they would only have the air in their suits to breathe and the light in the forward emergency generators. Diego did not know how long that would supply them with power.

Then came a shock wave, shaking them like a cat shakes a mouse, even those in safety restraints. Cries of pain and surprise echoed through the control room. Was that the other part of the ship? Had it exploded on the other side or this side of the portal?

"Communications?"

"No systems, sir. Communications aren't responding."

"*Dios mio!*" Diego cried in frustration. Now their only hope was in someone on Amashi seeing them on their monitors. "The people below?"

We made it, Diego. Captain Tremorin and the others did it! They blew away the aft section and set off the explosives.

Fress, are there any injuries?

Other than being tossed around in the elevator, we are fine. That last jolt must have been a shock wave reaching us even through the portal.

Fress's infectious enthusiasm triggered Diego's smile. *I hope it was.*

We are stuck here, though. No power. We could climb out, but there would be nowhere to go. At least we are through the gate.

Yes, we are. Can you contact Bress? We have no communicator.

No, but I will keep trying. Trilenn says there is a forward light that works in emergency situations. You could flash it in the Seressin distress code. It's a small orange switch on the communications console.

Diego knew that code. They taught him early in his squire training. "Rreengrol, you remember the Seressin emergency code?"

"Of course I do."

Diego told him what to look for, and his Grrlock friend "swam" over to the communications console. He shared the seat with the Trolog communications officer and showed him the sequences. After several times, Rreengrol came back to the command chair while the Trolog repeated the sequences.

"Send a signal once every half meka dron," Diego said. Every five minutes, his mind translated. The Trolog shrugged assent, hunched over the board.

Now, all they could do was wait. It seemed forever, but his command chair told him only half an hour had passed. Then an hour, then another hour. Was it his imagination, or did the lights seem a little dimmer? Diego checked his suit. Another few hours of air. He would have thought the oxygen packs held more. He didn't think there would be any rescue happening in that short a time, but he'd keep hoping.

Then he saw the flashing of something shooting across the monitor. It came back, and Diego recognized it as a Seressin scout craft. It stayed with them, and he heard Fress cheering in his mind. Apparently, Bress was on board.

Yes! Yes! He is.

Diego tried direct communication with the other Turengen. *Can you hear me, Bress?*

Yes, Commander!

Can that craft do a magnetic beam tow? We don't have a great deal of air.

Yes, Commander, we can. What is your air situation?

Air for about a hundred and fifty meka drons.

Not much. We will tow you to Amashi. It will take a short time to accelerate, but it can be done.

Thanks!

Diego felt the soft jerk as beams found a place on the mangled wreck. Then came the tug of the other ship towing what was left of *Revenge*. Several times, he felt a slight movement under his feet as the ship sped up. A study of his computer confirmed what his body felt. They were speeding toward Amashi.

Diego again admonished everyone to conserve their air as best as they could. It became hard to sit without moving. Rreengrol floated beside him, curled up, napping. All Diego wanted to do was pace. Of course, he couldn't do that either. So, he relaxed in the restraints of his chair.

The atmosphere buffeted the ship, but the link to their rescuers was tight. Diego watched as they slowed to land. He knew it would be tricky, but Bress and his crew could do it.

When they touched down, all he could do was sigh. Even that was hard to do. Diego's air was almost gone. Some of the crew experienced the torpor of low oxygen levels. Diego gazed at the sky and wondered, sleepily, if he was underwater. Everything looked strange and fuzzy. At the bump of their landing, he staggered to the emergency access, unsealing the hatchway. "Rreengrol." There was no answer. He looked around and found his friend curled under the navigational console, unconscious. Diego had to get the hatch open.

He half slid and half climbed down the ladder. Diego pushed several times before the small door opened. He unsealed his helmet and let the warm, fresh air greet him. His lungs sucked it in, reveling in the salty scent. Diego pushed the door open as far as it could go and almost fell into the arms of one of the Amashi robots. Bress, Rrishan, and Jeng leaped out of their ship.

"Commander!" Rrishan shouted. There were several Seressin, Breanth, and Treesh squires accompanying them.

"There are twenty-five crewmembers inside, including seven or eight stuck inside the elevator. Some will need medical attention," Diego gasped as he sucked in the wonderful air.

Rrishan and the squires hurried past Diego and into the battered, truncated craft. Soon, they brought the Trolog crewmembers out, handing them over to the Amashi three-legged robots. Diego tried to order the one attending him away to help the others, but the robot ignored him.

"Are you all right, Sub-Commander?" a gravelly voice asked.

Diego looked up and saw a Seressin sub-commander. He thought he looked familiar with purplish cheek patches underscored with red. "Yes, I am," he said, shaking his head to clear the lack of oxygen from his brain. "Sub-Commander Zengol, right?"

"Yes, Commander. Marix Ziron sent me out and gave me clearance to assist you."

"As soon as I can walk to my craft, I will report to the commander."

The Seressin nodded. "He would like that. He was most interested in your well-being."

Diego smiled. "By the barest margins and by whatever deities look after fools and space travelers, we made it back."

Zengol glanced at the battered craft. "I believe you are right, Sub-Commander. It is a miracle this hunk of junk made it through a portal."

"And the remainder of the ship did not."

Zengol studied the remains of the Trolog ship. "Specifically, the engine room?"

"Yes. Dangerous weaponry filled the rest of the ship." Diego studied the wreck and was astonished. He would have to thank the cutters and Tendar, Tremorin, Trell, and Trilenn for finishing the job.

"No propulsion. Amazing," Zengol growled.

"No choice, either. It was that or splatter Amashi into little bits of space dust."

The Seressin's distaste was apparent. "Wet space dust."

Diego grinned. "I suppose so." He walked back to the ship and helped pull the rest of the crew from *Revenge*.

Rreengrol was under the care of Rrishan and awake enough to not like it. "Are you all right?" she asked her brother.

"Except for my pelt turned inside out and my tail coming out of my nose, I'm fine," Rreengrol said. "I really am fine. I made it through another adventure with my favorite human."

Diego laughed. "I'm the only human you know. But we made it. We actually made it."

"And since when don't your crazy ideas make it?" Rreengrol stood up, shaking off the dust. Rrishan stuck to his side. "I'm all right, sib!" he told her.

"Still…" Rrishan began.

Rreengrol rolled his eyes.

"I need to find Fress. She was amazing on this trip." Diego heard some chittering nearer the ship.

Bress called out to him. "We are over here, Commander."

Diego approached the group. Her teammates patted and preened Fress as they examined her. She was making purring noises he had never heard before. "Are you all right, Fress?"

"Oh, yes. And we are here and all alive."

Diego nodded. "We sure are!"

Tremorin limped toward him. The Trolog captain had two black eyes, scratches, and a torn uniform. "Commander?"

"You and your team did a wonderful job! Thank you, Captain. You are limping."

Tremorin nodded. "Sore knee. If I was honest, I'd have to tell you I didn't think this was going to work."

"But we had to try."

CHAPTER FORTY-SIX

"We did, but how am I going to get back to Treela?" Then his frown turned into a smile. "I didn't think I was going to be alive to ask that question."

"I must talk with my commanding officer and give him a report. In the meantime, you may all stay in the rest center. You'll be able to get some well-deserved sleep, and you, and anyone else with injuries, will get medical care."

"Although we were going to blast the Amashi system out of existence?"

"The Amashi don't care, and neither do the robots," Diego stated. "And it was the Dominar who planned Amashi's destruction, not you."

Several hours later, Diego sat in the communications center, in contact with High Commander Ziron. Zengol waited nearby, ready to give his report as well.

"I send you on a simple diplomatic mission, and you almost blow up a portal and destroy an alien ship," he growled.

Diego was speechless. Commander Ziron's reprimands could be blistering. Then he saw his marix's toothy grin, and Diego realized he wasn't angry.

"Report, Sub-Commander!"

"Yes, sir." Diego gave a detailed overview of his activities since his last report.

"And so, you have twenty-two displaced alien warriors under your care."

"Yes, sir."

"Do you think they are a threat to the Seressin Empire?"

"Marix, I don't think the Trologs are an immediate threat,

either these or the ones back on their planet. I could be mistaken, but the Trolog captain said this was their only usable spaceship. They stockpiled all their weaponry in it. Their planet is almost unlivable. If there is an unknown factor, it's the Dominar. He is the leader of the main Trolog city."

"It sounds as though this Dominar put all of his hatchlings into one nursery," Ziron murmured.

"Yes, sir, I think he did, but he could still be dangerous, especially if he can put together another spaceship. The spaceport, if you could call it that, had many parts. And the Dominar's scientists will make more weapons if they can gather the materials."

"Yes, that's a valid point. You and Sub-Commander Zengol will return the Trolog nationals to their planet. Of course, that's after they recuperate and benefit from the generosity of the Seressin Empire for a reasonable time. Perhaps these Trologs will want to try an alliance with us." Ziron paused, closing his eyes for a moment and scratching his cheek patch. His eyes snapped back open. "An alliance would allow us to keep a close watch on them and exert some small measure of control against planetary annihilation. Such power in the hands of someone like you have described would make even the Supreme Commander quake." The High Commander leaned closer to the screen. "I trust you not to repeat that."

Diego nodded his head. That was indeed a bold admission.

"Try to discover what this Dominar is doing now — how much power he has and what kind of threat he is to the Empire. It sounds as though allying with these Trolog rebels would be most helpful for us. If, after you return to Trolog, you think it would be profitable for the Empire, then discuss with the outlander leadership what we could do to help them. I will send you an outline of the protocol for approaching a new system and a new star-faring people.

"At the very least, we'll be able to monitor them from now on. And determine if their system is inside the Seressin Empire. If not, claim it. We don't want the Resh to snatch this system. That these Trologs figured out a planetary portal is disturbing enough without it being under enemy control."

Diego was ready for this assignment to end. "Yes, sir. Then we will return to the *Star Devourer*?"

Ziron frowned. "I'm not done, Sub-Commander Diego."

Diego felt the heat rise under his collar. "Sorry, sir."

"Then you and your crew will return to Amashi and finish your leave."

"Sir?"

"You heard me, Quirlis! Have a restful time. Just don't try talking me into coming to Amashi."

"Yes, sir!"

CHAPTER FORTY-SEVEN

After being rescued, Captain Tremorin and the others healed and rested for almost a week. Some took excursions in the ocean.

Diego and Tremorin walked along one of the many beaches, watching the waves splash over their feet. After his talk with Marix Ziron, Diego wanted to know the captain's feelings about the Dominar but didn't know how to bring it up. The Dominar would most likely punish Tremorin, but did the captain still feel loyal to his leader? Diego took a deep breath. "What will you do when you get home to Trolog?"

Tremorin stopped and gazed out over the vast ocean. "I don't know. The Dominar will probably want my head. Treela and her mother will be in danger, too. I hate that more than anything."

Diego thought about Treela, and Tremorin's words faded. He pictured her smooth skin, her beautiful green eyes, and her long, expressive fingers. He wanted to see her again. Then he questioned himself. Was it because she looked like him? Those things drew him to her in the beginning, despite her quirks and moodiness. Still, he shuddered at the thought of living on Trolog. Nothing about the planet enticed him.

His thoughts raced around in his head like the squirrels running up and down the tree trunks back on Earth. Diego pushed those thoughts from his mind. "What about the outlanders? I know Tendar said you were welcome to live with them and become a part of their colony."

"Joining with the outlanders will be our only option. We'll be in hiding." Tremorin sighed.

Diego paused before speaking his next thought. "It seemed

more like hiding in your city than in the outlander's dwellings. At least to me."

Tremorin stopped and gazed at him. "You have seen the outlander settlements. I haven't. Is it livable?"

"Captain, many of the outlanders are scientists and skilled workers who are against the Dominar's policies. Or he imprisoned them for speaking against him. They used their expertise to create comfortable quarters underground." Diego dug his toes into the sand. "I can't imagine the Dominar will stay in power for long after this. I know little about politics, but I know you can't use all your resources on weapons and spaceships. And you can't let your people go hungry without those people finally getting angry with their leaders."

Tremorin shook his head. "I know there were some rumblings of discontent, but the Dominar is slippery and remains in power, even though people are unhappy with him."

"The outlanders are very advanced, too. If they had the materials, I believe they could build a new spaceship."

Tremorin studied Diego. "I think I can understand why your commander gave you important missions, even at such a youthful age. You have made several viable points. If they'll let me, I'd like to help them." Tremorin waded out into the warm waters. "I want to work to bring Trolog back to what it was." He walked out deep enough to paddle around. One of the Amashina swam a little closer to the shore but not near enough to interfere.

Diego felt a light touch on his ear and shivered. Rrishan tickled him with the tip of her tail. "A message from the Amashina or a request from Commander Ziron?"

"Neither. I just wanted to come out and enjoy the sunset with you, Sub-Commander Diego."

He turned with a smile. "Sunsets are nice to enjoy with a friend." Rrishan stood close, closer than usual. Diego could feel the heat of her body, and he didn't find it at all unpleasant. "We'll be going back to Trolog in a day."

Rrishan said nothing for several long moments. Tremorin still splashed out in the ocean, watching a few ocean fish glowing in the water as the light faded. "These Trologs are very much like you. I mean, they look like you."

Diego nodded and lowered his voice. "I know, but Trolog is not a nice place to live."

"You were thinking of staying there?" Her voice quavered.

"I don't know. Like you said, they look like me."

A soft rumble rose in Rrishan's throat. Diego recognized it as her empathy sound. The hum continued as the breezes cooled him in the growing darkness. "A creature doesn't have to look like you to be a pleasant companion." Her yellow-green eyes continued to gaze at the spot where the sun had set.

"I know."

"Even though you may believe you're alone here in the Empire, you're not alone." Rrishan continued gazing toward the ocean.

"I know that, too."

They said nothing for a few minutes. Rrishan sighed. "I'm going in. The breezes have picked up."

Diego laughed. "Since when has a little breeze bothered Squire Rrishan? You have a nice soft layer of fur."

The tail tickled his ear again, and then she sprinted up the beach to the guest houses.

"That was one tickle too many!" Diego chased after her but then remembered Captain Tremorin was still out in the water. While he knew the Amashina looked out for the Trolog, Diego thought it would be the height of rudeness to leave him. With a sigh, he turned back to the shore.

Tremorin watched him. "I'm glad you didn't leave me behind. I forgot my flashlight. The water is soothing and refreshing, and the underwater creatures are fascinating, but I lost track of the time."

"I understand. Sometimes, I have been swimming and didn't want to come back to land."

"To chase Trologs?"

Diego smiled but said nothing.

Tremorin gazed at the shifting colors of the ocean and the brightness of the stars overhead. "Amazing how things have changed in just a short time."

"Yes, sir, it is."

"How soon can I return to my daughter? And will it be through the portal or on a ship?"

Diego felt the ocean breezes ruffling his hair. He stroked the fuzz above his lip. "Definitely in a ship. You wouldn't want to come out on the other side of the sea portal. Besides, the robots would have to make twenty-two underwater suits for you and your people."

Tremorin laughed. "Hmm, valid point."

"Also, the sea portal comes out near Trologar, so going by ship would be much safer for everyone. We will leave tomorrow at sunset."

"Good. I'm ready to go home. And figure out a way to get my wife out of Trologar," Tremorin said, as they returned to their quarters.

———

With his crew, Diego made the return trip to Trolog without incident. Tendar gave the navigator the coordinates, and they landed in a valley near one of the outlander cities. Diego watched the monitor for any activity from the Dominar. Tendar signaled the nearest outlander post.

"Communication from the Trolog outlander base," Rrishan reported. "They are allowing refuge for the crew of the *Revenge* but request we return to orbit as soon as they have disembarked."

"Acknowledge." Diego turned to Rreengrol. "I am going

to accompany Tendar and the others to make sure they are safe. I also need to convey a message from Commander Ziron."

"Who will accompany you?" Rreengrol asked.

"Fress."

The Turengen beamed and slid from her seat, her whiskers shaking with pleasure. "I am ready, Commander."

Diego took his communicator to summon the ship back when they were ready to leave.

"We will let you know if there is any movement from Trologar," Rrishan told him.

"Good. When you return to orbit, check on the spaceport. Let me know if there's any activity there." Diego didn't think the Dominar could do anything right now but put nothing past him.

"Be careful, Diego, uh, Commander," Rrishan murmured as he headed out of the control room.

He locked eyes with her for a brief second, nodding to acknowledge her concern.

Sub-Commander Zengol closed the hatch behind them. The ship had lifted off by the time Diego and Fress reached the entrance to the outlander city. As the outside door closed behind them, Diego saw Treela wrapped in her father's arms. He smiled.

After a few minutes, she spied him and dashed in his direction. Diego found himself wrapped in a bear hug, a choke hold on his neck. He hugged her back. After several minutes, she slid down and gazed at him. "Thanks for bringing back Father."

"You're welcome."

"Are you going to help us overthrow the Dominar?"

Diego felt off-center and didn't know what to say, at least until he fulfilled Commander Ziron's orders.

Treela backed up a step and studied him.

"I need to speak with outlander leadership and pass along a message from Commander Ziron. Then I can think about what you've asked."

"If he's not stopped, he'll destroy the planet," Treela insisted.

"He might if he had the resources."

Treela frowned. She turned to her father, but he only shrugged.

Diego felt a bit of irritation at the captain. "You know I have to follow orders."

Tremorin nodded. He put his arm around his daughter and led her away. "Let's go, and I can tell you what happened after *Revenge* took off."

Treela turned and glared at Diego. "You look like us. You don't look like those commanders of yours. Don't you think you should help us, people who are like you?" Her father escorted her down the corridor.

Diego stared after them and sighed.

Fress joined Diego. *I think Treela seriously likes you.*

I already knew that, Diego snapped. *You don't have to be telepathic all the time.*

Fress ignored the last comment. *Are you? Going to stay, that is.*

I'm a member of the Seressin Empire and a sub-commander under Commander Ziron.

Fress snorted. *You think Commander Ziron wouldn't let you resign?*

Diego didn't know what to think. He didn't want to stay on this war-blasted planet, but Treela was right about one thing—he resembled the Trologs. *I think Commander Ziron would not be happy with me for submitting a resignation.*

You could figure out a way if you wanted to.

An outlander broke into his thoughts. "Do you want dinner, sir?"

Diego's stomach rumbled. How long had he stood there thinking? "Yes, I would." The outlander led him and Fress further down the corridor. They arrived at a cavernous room where a large group of people ate and talked.

When Diego picked up his bowl of stew along with a hunk of round bread, he sat down on a stone block. He scooped up a spoonful of the food. It steamed, and Diego blew on it.

Treela approached him, put down her dish, then sat facing him. "I'm sorry for what I said earlier."

Diego took a couple of bites before he said anything. "I understand your feelings."

"Then why don't you help us?"

With a sigh, Diego set his spoon down and tried to pull together his confused thoughts. "Treela, I must talk to the leaders here, and then I can give you more details. I am a junior commander in the Seressin Empire and am under orders."

Treela grimaced. "Why would you feel obligated to the people who snatched you away from your home?"

Diego wondered the same thing for a moment. "What you say is true, but these are also the people who taught me and gave me my rank and warrior status."

Treela stared at him. "Don't you realize you could do so much to help our people?"

"I will talk to the outland leaders and find out if there could be any alliances."

"Alliances with such different creatures?"

Diego nodded. "Yes. Why not? They accepted me and Fress and Rrishan. You felt that. I thought you liked the idea of working with different people."

Treela turned away, staring down at her bowl but not eating anything. "It's so hard."

———

Several days later, Diego stood at the edge of the cliff, watching the sun sink like a ball of liquid fire beyond a far mountain range. His thoughts churned. He couldn't put together any coherent words to convey to Treela what he had to do.

"Diego." Treela lay her hand on his shoulder, her other arm reaching around his waist.

He felt the heat of her presence.

"You're not staying, are you?" She sniffed, and her voice trembled.

"No, just as I don't think you could leave Trolog." Diego had asked her to come back with him and learn more about the Seressin Empire.

Treela pulled back. "How do you know that? I still might."

Diego shook his head. "No. You are tied to the Trolog of your past."

She pushed him around to face her. "And what's wrong with that?" she snapped.

Diego remembered Rrishan's comments as they returned to Trolog. 'Are you sure you could remain on Trolog?' No, he wasn't sure. Rrishan's soft, trilling purr not only showed her sadness but also her respect for his choice — whatever it might be.

"No, there's nothing wrong with wanting Trolog the way it used to be. I would love to see your world other than scorched earth and rocks."

She reached her hands around his waist again. "We could see it change together."

Diego felt her touch but wondered again about being stuck on Trolog for the rest of his life. It didn't appeal. Then he thought of his longing for Earth. He contemplated spending his life working on a ranch in the hills and realized such a life didn't appeal to him, either. So, what did he want? He realized he wanted acceptance. Wherever he ended up, he desired to be accepted.

When he didn't answer, she pulled away. "It's all about your reptile master," she snapped and then covered her mouth with one hand.

Diego frowned. "He is hard to get to know but is fair in his own way. And he is my commander, not my master." Diego thought of Fuerte, Phris, and the Turengens. And Rreengrol and Rrishan. "Not my master. I am not a slave!"

"Diego, I didn't mean what I said."

He knew Treela still found the various creatures strange and somehow inferior. It had taken him a while to get used to all the physical and mental differences in his comrades. Treela would, too. But it wouldn't be by leaving Trolog. She remained as tied to her world as Diego was to his. He gazed into Treela's green eyes. Before he could react, she pulled him close and kissed him. He felt her warm lips and body. His resolve didn't waver.

Then she pulled away, gazing into his eyes until she turned and ran back into the outlander cave. By now, the sun had set, and the darkness surrounded him like a blanket. He thought back to the time he spent on Grrlock. Lershan, Rreengrol, and Rrishan. It felt like being part of a family. The Turengens, Phris, and even Ziron, in his own way, were like a family.

Diego looked up at the murky sky, trying to find a few stars. He saw a few anemically filtered until they looked like faded and sick fireflies. Then he blinked, and they disappeared. Diego knew he couldn't stay here. Even if these people looked like him. That wasn't enough. Rebuilding a world? A worthy endeavor, but not his endeavor. Something else waited for him.

He finished negotiating with the outlander leadership for support from, as well as an alliance with, the Seressin Empire, all to neutralize the Dominar. The outlanders impressed Diego with their abilities. With their smarts and the empire helping them, Trolog would rise from their disastrous past. What they had already built underground impressed him.

What would the Seressins get from it? Portal technology. The portal from Amashi to Trolog, planet to planet, intrigued Ziron and the Supreme Commander. And the outlanders gave the empire permission to build a base to help the reptilians monitor the Resh or anyone else interested in Trolog technology. He smiled. That would aggravate the Dominar.

A glow burnished the eastern horizon — the first moon was about to rise. Diego coughed as some of the dust particles tickled his throat. No, he wanted to go home, the home he had made among his friends. He would return with Rreengrol, Rrishan, Zengol, and the Turengen. He would return to his home.

Diego pushed the call button on his communicator.

Susan Kite was born in Indiana, but because her father was in the Army, she moved extensively during her growing-up years. The post library was the first place she found after a move, avidly reading fantasy, science fiction, and many other genres. In her teens, she dabbled in writing, creating stories based on characters from her favorite TV shows. With college and marriage, writing was mostly put on hold.

That changed more than twenty years ago when the writing bug bit again. For a decade, fan fiction was the main focus, but this provided practice and helped develop the skills needed to write original works. A visit to the Mission San Luis Rey in California in 2001 and subsequent research became the catalyst to write her first novel, *My House of Dreams. The Mendel Experiment* and its sequels, *Blue Fire and Power Stone of Alogol,* were published by World Castle.

The author earned her Bachelor's degree in secondary

English and followed that up with a Master's degree in Instructional Media at Utah State University. She worked in public school libraries for 35 years, most recently in Chattanooga, Tennessee. Now retired, Ms. Kite lives in Oklahoma City. She has been married to the love of her life, Daniel, for over 40 years. They have two children and seven grandchildren and are owned by an opinionated chiweenie-terrier.